Five years hadn't

Dark eyes and w... full of angles—sharp ...ght blade of a nose. H... ...lipped and broad shouldered, dressed all in black right down to the Stetson he clutched in one hand. No doubt, he was an excellent-looking man on the surface, except that all Fleur could see in front of her was a coldhearted monster.

Even his smile looked more like a baring of white teeth as he spoke. "Miss Colorado Silver Spurs and I are well acquainted, Marta."

Fleur's grip on the work application tightened so hard the form crumpled in her fist. Which was just as well. Better to have her dreams go belly-up than have her life destroyed by this man yet again.

* * *

Rocky Mountain Rivals by Joanne Rock
is part of the Return to Catamount series.

Dear Reader,

We all know someone who isn't speaking to a family member. Maybe you're that someone! Fleur Barclay knows how much that hurts, and so does her whole family. Sometimes a falling-out is so embedded into a clan that no one knows quite how to cross the divide.

But Fleur has never totally given up on her siblings or her parents. She may not be the middle child, but she's the one most likely to reach out. To try again. To keep on loving through rejection. In the world we live in, qualities like Fleur's can sometimes be overlooked as "weaknesses," but to me, they look like deep-seated goodness that deserves some love in return.

Enter her longtime rival! Who would have expected that she'd find romance in the place she least expected? In Catamount, Colorado, where she's long been misperceived? But Drake Alexander knows more about Fleur than he's letting on, because he's been watching out for her from the sidelines even when she didn't appreciate it one bit.

I hope you enjoy *Rocky Mountain Rivals*, the first book in my new Return to Catamount series from Harlequin Desire!

Happy reading!

Joanne Rock

JOANNE ROCK

—

ROCKY MOUNTAIN RIVALS

HARLEQUIN®
DESIRE™

Recycling programs
for this product may
not exist in your area.

ISBN-13: 978-1-335-73566-9

Rocky Mountain Rivals

Copyright © 2022 by Joanne Rock

For questions and comments about the quality of this book, please contact us at CustomerService@Harlequin.com.

Harlequin Enterprises ULC
22 Adelaide St. West, 41st Floor
Toronto, Ontario M5H 4E3, Canada
www.Harlequin.com

Printed in U.S.A.

Joanne Rock credits her decision to write romance after a book she picked up during a flight delay engrossed her so thoroughly that she didn't mind at all when her flight was delayed two more times. Giving her readers the chance to escape into another world has motivated her to write over eighty books for a variety of Harlequin series.

Books by Joanne Rock

Harlequin Desire

Dynasties: Mesa Falls

Return to Catamount

Visit her Author Profile page at Harlequin.com, or joannerock.com, for more titles.

You can also find Joanne Rock on Facebook, along with other Harlequin Desire authors, at Facebook.com/harlequindesireauthors!

For my friends and readers
with complicated family dynamics.
Wishing you peace and patience to heal
where you can and wisdom to set
boundaries when you can't.

One

She hoped it was a good omen.

Lured by the Help Wanted sign in the window of the one and only restaurant in Catamount, Colorado, Fleur Barclay stepped out of her beat-up car to inquire inside. The heat of the summer sun warmed her face; the scent of barbecue carried on the breeze. The Cowboy Kitchen was a local institution that had been in business when Fleur and her family used to visit her grandmother in Catamount when she was a kid. The restaurant had remained a local staple through her teen years when Fleur had been the only Barclay still visiting Gran after her parents split and her sisters had chosen sides in the acrimonious divorce.

Now, five years removed from when Fleur fled this small town in the wake of an unhappy split of her own, she was heartened to see Cowboy Kitchen still in business. And in need of help.

Given that she was currently unemployed and needed to remain in town until she settled her grandmother's estate, Fleur chose to view the ad as a sign that her recent string of bad luck was changing.

The past few months had brought her beloved Gran's passing, and a spate of inappropriate advances by her boss that had made her work life impossible. She'd felt forced to leave her assistant chef position. The only tiny silver lining? At least she could live on her Gran's ranch while she readied the place for sale. She wouldn't have been able to pay her rent in Dallas for much longer anyhow, especially since finding a good gig in Texas would have been a challenge without her boss's recommendation.

Something she'd obviously never receive since she'd filed a discrimination complaint with the State.

Unwilling to think about that now, Fleur skirted through a handful of parked cars in front of the lodge-style building that housed a small hardware store and a post office service window in addition to the eatery. Well, *diner*, really. But she could hardly afford to be choosy when the place was just a few miles from Crooked Elm, Gran's ranch. She needed an income to pay her bills. She couldn't bear the thought of touching the savings earmarked for opening her own restaurant one day. And "one day" might come all the sooner if she could make enough from the sale of her grandmother's property.

A rusted bell chimed overhead as she stepped

through the entrance. The scent of bacon hung heavy in the air even though it was long past noon. The decor remained the same as ever—white countertops, black-and-white laminate floors, chrome barstools with turquoise seats from a bygone era. The only thing remotely Western about the Cowboy Kitchen was the oversize painting of a faded brown Stetson on the wall above the counter. If there'd been a lunch crowd, it had since departed. A couple of old-timers dressed in faded coveralls sat at a table near the window, hunched over coffee cups. Another patron—younger but dressed like the others in boots and denim—scrolled through his phone at the counter.

"Be right with you!" A feminine voice called from somewhere in the back, probably in response to the doorbell.

Smoothing her blue cotton skirt wrinkled from travel, Fleur moved closer to the counter where a sleek computer monitor sat beside a simple credit card reader. The decor might be from another era, but someone had clearly upgraded the tech. Was that another good sign that a chef role would pay a reasonable wage? Fleur already knew there was no cash in Gran's estate, so until she could sell the Crooked Elm and split the proceeds evenly with her older sisters, she needed to be careful of her expenses.

And wasn't that the same as ever? Her property developer father had cut her off financially the day she'd turned eighteen, perceiving Fleur's efforts at smoothing the family rifts to be "taking her mother's side" in the never-ending divorce war. The feud was so over-the-top it would be laughable if it weren't heartbreaking at the same time. Another frustration she shoved to the back of her mind.

"And…how can I help you?" A smiling brunette pushed her way through the white swinging door from the kitchen to greet her. "Table for one?"

The woman had bright pink lipstick and an abundance of freckles, her dark hair in a long ponytail. She wore an all-white uniform with a silver name tag that read "Marta."

That's right. Marta Macon. Her family lived on the outskirts of town. Fleur thought her dad might work at the hardware store.

"Actually, no. I was here about the sign in the window. Are you still hiring?" Fleur knew certain people in Catamount would view a diner job in her grandmother's rural hometown as a step down for her. Plenty of locals knew the great lengths she'd gone to in order to earn enough money for culinary school tuition.

Some of her peers had deemed entering regional pageants to earn scholarships as "giving herself airs." One man in particular had scoffed at her path, spouting tired opinions about rodeo pageants reinforcing gendered power dynamics and contributing to the objectification of women. Easy for wealthy Drake Alexander to judge her when he'd never had to worry about paying his own way for anything.

And just how had Drake crept into her thoughts after all this time? She chased him out of her head.

"We are most definitely hiring." Marta bent to retrieve a paper from beneath the counter while a Patsy Cline tune played on an overhead speaker. "You're one of the Barclay girls, aren't you?"

"That's right. I'm Fleur." She smiled politely, though she wasn't sure many people would recall her older sisters since neither Lark nor Jessamyn had spent time in Catamount for years. "We were in 4-H together."

Crooked Elm Ranch had been her summer home every year until she'd finished high school. Then she'd spent two straight years living in Colorado, working multiple jobs to save enough for culinary school.

Until she'd had no choice but to leave.

"I remember you. Have you waitressed before?"

"Yes." Was there any support role she hadn't taken in the restaurant world? "But I hoped you might need help on the cook staff."

"Sorry." The other woman shook her head, dark ponytail shadowing her movements as she began straightening some napkins spilling out of a dispenser. "We're all set in the kitchen. Stella McRory never misses a shift, and she's been here longer than I have."

"Oh." She couldn't hide her disappointment. Not that she objected to food service. But the public-facing position would practically ensure she'd have to smile at too many people she hoped never to see again. Mostly Drake Alexander. "I'll have to think about it, in that case. Do you mind if I take the form?"

There would only be so much work available around town, after all. In another couple of weeks, she wouldn't have the option to be choosy when her savings dwindled.

"Sure thing." Marta moved on to the next napkin dispenser, straightening the paper products. "Just swing by with it if you decide to apply. It's a fun place to work. Everybody stops in sooner or later."

Just as she feared.

Fleur backed up a step, folding the application in half. Before she could reply, Marta continued.

"And the working environment has gotten nicer since the diner changed hands. The new owner is great. I even have a 401(k) now," Marta announced proudly, hands flying from one dispenser to the next, prepping for the dinner crowd with practiced ease.

The thought of a savings account had Fleur rethinking her need to work in a kitchen.

"Really? Who owns the place these days?" Unfolding the application again, she smoothed out the wrinkles as she studied the paper for a clue to the new management.

Behind her, the old-fashioned doorbell chimed. Marta's expression brightened.

"Here's the owner now," she offered in a cheery voice, gesturing toward the entrance.

Fleur turned expectantly.

And any hopes of her luck changing took a nosedive.

Seeing the imposing frame and chiseled features

of the most unfeeling bastard she'd ever met, her chances for a job expired on the spot.

Marta, unaware, continued, "Do you remember Drake Alexander from your time in Catamount? He's our local rodeo star."

Fleur seemed to hear the words as if they were spoken from far away, her full attention locked on the man responsible for driving her from town five years ago. He'd always disliked her. Then, when she'd started dating Drake's younger brother, the enmity had redoubled.

Five years hadn't changed her nemesis.

Dark eyes and dark, waving hair that framed a face full of angles—sharp cheekbones, square chin, straight blade of a nose. He was slim hipped and broad shouldered, dressed all in black right down to the Stetson he clutched in one hand. No doubt, he was an excellent-looking man on the surface, except that all Fleur could see in front of her was a cold heart.

Even his smile looked more like a baring of white teeth as he spoke. "Miss Colorado Silver Spurs and I are well acquainted, Marta."

Fleur's grip on the work application tightened so hard the form crumpled in her fist. Which was just as well. Better to have her dreams go belly-up than subject herself to this man again. She jammed the ruined paper into the pocket of her jean jacket. Vaguely, she registered Marta saying something near them— but her focus remained on the man who'd broken up her engagement to his brother.

"How unfortunate to see you again, Drake," she said mildly, reminding herself she'd prepared for this moment. She'd understood that running into him again in this small town was inevitable. Thankfully, she didn't have to worry about seeing Colin in town since her former fiancé had relocated to Montana. "But at least now I know to avoid this place while I'm in Catamount for the summer."

"Hoping to recapture the old glory as rodeo royalty? Or are you leaving the field clear for newcomers?"

He wasted no time returning to their old antagonism. But then, that way it was easier for her to deal with the complicated feelings this man had always stirred inside her.

"I might ask you the same question. I hear your rodeo days are as far in the past as my pageants. But as much fun as it would be to chat about all the ways you torpedoed my life, I have places to be." She hitched the strap of her purse higher on one shoulder and turned toward Marta. "It was nice seeing you again, Marta."

Breezing past the tall, rangy form of Drake Alexander with a cool disdain at odds with the fiery anger inside her, Fleur shoved open the door of the Cowboy Kitchen and vowed never to enter the building again.

Inside the Cowboy Kitchen, Drake dropped into the booth closest to the door and told himself not to look out the front window to see where Fleur Barclay had gone.

Unfortunately, his eyes were already glued to her slender frame as she glided between the parked cars to wrench open the reluctant door of a compact rust bucket old enough to be a certifiable antique. Not exactly the ride he would have expected for the former rodeo queen, but then nothing about Fleur played to type.

Damn, but she looked more incredible than ever.

No amount of beauty, though, could cover a greedy heart. He resented her for trying to trap his younger brother into marriage, after dating only a couple of months. And even before then, he'd found plenty of reasons to avoid her.

But there was no denying that Fleur turned heads. His included. With endless legs and lips so full they launched torrid fantasies before she ever opened her mouth, Fleur appealed to him as much as she ticked him off. It was an awkward combination that meant he'd kept his distance from her. Especially when she was seven years younger and firmly off limits when they'd repeatedly run into one another on the rodeo circuit.

Until he'd found out about the sudden unwise engagement to his brother when she'd been just twenty years old. As de facto head of the Alexander family since his parents' deaths, Drake took his role in protecting his siblings seriously. So he'd told Fleur exactly what he thought of her marriage ploy. And within days, her engagement to his brother had ended, and Colin—blaming Drake for the split—had moved to Montana. Drake had hoped the anger his brother felt about his interference would fade, but in five years, Colin hadn't returned home once.

Now, watching Fleur step into her vehicle, Drake eyed the way her short blue skirt hugged her hips. A trio of silver necklaces caught the June sunlight where they dangled on the front of her plain white T, a fringed jean jacket the only nod to her old rodeo queen days.

A heavy mug clunked down onto the table in front of him, breaking his reverie. Marta stood beside his booth and filled the stoneware cup from a steaming glass pot, releasing the scent of coffee into the air.

"I would have given my right arm to be the national Miss Silver Spurs," she informed him with a sniff. "The horsemanship skills in that competition are very well respected."

"I'm sure they are," he acknowledged, guilt nipping his conscience. "I meant no offense to the rodeo pageants—"

"It sure sounded like you did," Marta shot back, her former sunny smile nowhere in sight. "Do you have any idea how many good works those women are involved in for their communities if they win?"

He did know, actually. And he needed to do better than to spout off like that just because Fleur had always gotten under his skin.

"I apologize. Fleur and I have a history and I shouldn't have spoken to her that way." He didn't want to rile his best waitress and manager. So he changed topics. "Did she say what she was here for, by the way?"

He guessed she'd come to town to settle her grandmother's estate. Hopefully, it would be the speediest process in the history of Catamount.

"She was looking for a job. But since she crumpled the application into pulp when she saw you, I doubt she'll be applying." Marta turned on a heel and stalked off to refill the cups of the only other diners in the establishment.

Fleur wanted a job?

Just how long was she planning on staying in Catamount?

He shouldn't have given in to the reflex to taunt her. Drake had been waiting for Crooked Elm to go up for sale for years. And now that it finally seemed like a viable possibility, his first move was to resort to sparring with Fleur a reflex from the old days when he'd worked hard to keep her at arm's length.

Why hadn't he offered her condolences about losing her grandmother? He'd always liked Antonia Barclay, even if she'd refused to sell him a key piece of her ranch property for years. She'd warned him that one day he would have to bargain with her granddaughters for the right to buy the land.

Now that day had come and he'd already started on the wrong foot. He'd just been caught off guard when he'd walked into the diner and saw a woman so gorgeous she'd sent a thrill through him. When she'd spun around enough that he'd recognized her...

All the old tangle of bitterness and hunger had him shoving his boot in his mouth.

He took a sip of the coffee and promptly scalded

his tongue. Drake swore softly and glanced out the front windows again.

The rust-bucket car was still parked there—right beside his pickup truck. Through the windshield, he could see Fleur in the driver's seat, head bent over her phone.

Before he could think the better of it, he shot to his feet and pushed his way out of the exit. He clapped his Stetson on his head midstride, then squared his shoulders to face her.

He wanted to offer to buy Crooked Elm then and there. She'd been very willing to accept a payout from an Alexander man five years ago during the engagement to Colin. He'd overheard them discussing a prenup—with substantial provisions for Fleur—before the engagement was a week old. It had rubbed him raw to have his brother tied down when Fleur hadn't even had the chance to attend culinary school yet, prompting his visit to Fleur to tell her exactly what he thought of it. And while their argument that night had been effective in encouraging her to break things off with his brother, it had also left a deep scar on his family.

He could acknowledge now that he'd mishandled things. He was wiser now. So maybe he could convince her to sell the ranch without ever having to list the property with a Realtor.

But the fact that she drove the beat-up car gave him pause. He'd written her off as a gold digger once upon a time. Yet that label didn't fit with the car she was driving. Or the fact that she'd been looking for a job at the Cowboy Kitchen of all places. It wasn't much as far as eateries went, but it was the only food establishment in all of Catamount, and Drake had been unwilling to let the place go under when the former owner couldn't make the mortgage payments anymore. He would never leave this town, which meant it made sense to invest in the place.

As his shadow fell across the windshield, Fleur looked up. She startled, dropping her phone before her gray eyes narrowed at him.

Still, she rolled down her window, the hand crank making it unnecessary to even turn on the engine.

"Did you think of a few more jabs?" she asked, blinking up at him in the sunlight.

He wouldn't rise to the bait. If there was any chance Fleur would sell to him, he couldn't fall into old habits.

"I'm sorry about your grandmother. Everyone liked Antonia."

Fleur's face fell. Whether from sadness at her loss or disappointment that he hadn't stuck to their usual script, he couldn't say.

"Thank you." The words were stiff. Forced. "I'll organize a memorial once I'm sure my sisters can be here."

He hadn't seen all three Barclay sisters in Catamount at the same time since he'd been a teen. He'd never forget the day, either. There'd been a junior rodeo at the county fair shortly after the elder Barclays' breakup. Fleur's mother arrived with her oldest daughter, while Fleur's father had been in attendance with his mistress. Jessamyn, the middle daughter, had been in a barrel racing competition. Drake had been in the stands watching since the bull riding event started later in the day.

Security had to get involved after the mistress—the wife of a prominent divorce attorney, of all things—used her designer purse like a medieval mace, knocking Mrs. Barclay down a few stairs. Fleur had been in the early days of her rodeo career, so she'd been maybe nine years old at the time. She'd been dressed in red, white and blue satin, seated on horseback in the arena with a few other flag bearers, preparing for the opening laps. But she'd surprised the crowd by breaking into a spontaneous solo rendition of "America the Beautiful" after the fight broke out. The decision had seemed an odd choice to a lot of folks, since her mother could have very well been injured at the time, although Drake had suspected she'd been trying to deflect attention from the scene.

Later, he'd second-guessed the opinion, especially as he'd watched her grow into a dedicated pageant contestant, travelling all over the west for a shot at a title.

But for the rest of Catamount, Fleur's reputation for being self-centered had only grown from that day at the junior rodeo. He wasn't going to think about that now when he needed to convince her to sell him Crooked Elm. The ranch's rangelands had been overused by their current tenant and needed serious intervention to restore the soil quality. Conserving the land—using it in a way that gave back instead of stripping it—had been a goal of his parents. For that reason, it was an even more important goal for him.

"I'm sure you'll have a big turnout for her," he told Fleur belatedly, still deciding the best way to proceed. Should he make the offer now? Or backtrack and try to smooth over her impression of him to boost the chances she'd agree to it? Swallowing his pride in one hard lump, he tried to adopt a reasonably pleasant tone. "Marta mentioned you were in the market for a job?"

She laughed. A brisk, mirthless *ha!* "Only until I found out who owns the place."

He leaned against his pickup truck parked beside her car, then crossed one boot over the other as he picked his words carefully. Marta's admonishment about his judgmental words had reminded him he had no business needling Fleur anymore. She wasn't a kid any longer, and he couldn't still claim to be reeling from his parents' death. Time to rein in the sniping.

"We could keep clear of each other. I rarely set foot in there anyhow."

"This conversation just gets weirder and weirder." She shook her head, copper-colored curls jiggling with the motion. "Is this some kind of trick to humiliate me down the road? Do you want to invite your rich friends to heckle me while I wait on them?"

"Hardly." He'd do his damnedest to keep his friends away from a mercenary beauty queen. "I bought the diner because it was a good business move, not because I frequent the place. Don't let me keep you away if you want to work there."

"Now I know it's a trick," she said drily, bending forward to retrieve the phone she'd dropped on the car's floorboards. She sat up, eyes flaming. "There's no chance you would do anything to help me after the way you broke up my engagement and chased me out of Catamount last time. You're probably just angling to find the fastest method to send me running out of town again."

"That's not true—" he began, but she continued as if he'd never interrupted.

"No doubt you could make my life a living hell if you were my boss, so I'll pass. Thanks just the same." She jammed the phone into a cupholder and rolled up her window, effectively ending their conversation.

As efforts to smooth things over with her went, it wasn't half-bad.

It'd been almost civil. Or as civil as things had ever been between him and Fleur.

Still, as he watched the rusty car disappear up the road, Drake guessed he'd have to dig deeper on his campaign to win her over if he ever wanted her to sell him her grandmother's land.

Two

Standing in the bright yellow kitchen where she'd spent many happy hours cooking with her grandmother, Fleur leaned a hip against the Mexican tile countertop and adjusted her tablet on its stand. The oldest of the sisters, Lark, had FaceTimed her to finalize details for Antonia Barclay's memorial. Fleur was grateful for the virtual company when the house at Crooked Elm seemed to echo with loneliness now that Gran wasn't there. Not to mention, talking to Lark kept her mind off Drake and the frustration of their unexpected encounter.

Had it been her imagination or had he made an overture to friendliness after all this time? She knew she had to be misreading the situation. Better to focus on her plans for Antonia's memorial.

How many times had she and Gran sat at the table in the blue painted chairs, taste-testing one another's recipes? She glanced up at the decorative plates hung on the arch above the copper apron sink, remembering taking them down one day to clean them. Gran had narrated where and when she'd acquired each one, reminiscing about meeting Fleur's long-deceased grandfather when they were teens, then traveling the country with him before they settled on his family's ranch in Catamount. Fleur had treasured every story, her inner romantic thrilling to the idea that marriage didn't have to be the war zone that her parents had created.

Tugging her attention away from the plates, she refocused on Lark's face framed on the tablet screen. A practicing therapist, her older sister had glossy dark hair, arrow straight and reaching midway down her back. She wore it in a long braid today and her green eyes had shadows beneath them as she packed toys in her work satchel after counseling children in her home office in Los Angeles. Fleur guessed Lark must have some upcoming appointments on the road if she was loading her travel bag. Lark consulted with a couple of local schools in addition to her practice at home.

"Are you sure you can't spend the night after the memorial?" Fleur asked her for the second time.

She ached for family now, even more than usual. While her relationship with both Lark and Jessamyn was strained she was more likely to have sway with the eldest. Lark didn't hold as much of a grudge about Fleur's efforts as family peacekeeper as Jessamyn.

"I wish I could." Lark scooped up the last of the toys, a rag doll and a stuffed puppy with floppy ears, then pitched them in her duffel bag. "But I've had to draw big-time boundaries to protect myself from the drama with Dad. And I'm sad enough about Gran without adding his inevitable BS to the day."

Fleur clamped her teeth around her lower lip to prevent herself from arguing. Her sister looked exhausted, and Fleur knew it would be tough for her to return to Catamount even without family dysfunction. Lark's hockey player ex-husband had purchased a ranch in Catamount where he'd planned to spend his retirement after his sports career ended—right next door to the Barclays. And although the marriage had fallen apart before that day had come, he still hadn't sold the place yet. Her very private sister hadn't shared the full scope of the breakup with Fleur, but she knew it had been bad.

And if there was one thing Fleur understood, it was a bad breakup. She bore the scars of hers to this day.

"I understand." She traced the pattern in one of the tiles on the countertop, her finger following the blue flower petals before outlining the green stems. "It's just so quiet here without Gran."

"I'm sorry." Setting down the bag of toys, Lark looked right at her, surely seeing the hurt Fleur couldn't begin to express. "It feels strange for me, too, seeing that bright, happy kitchen without her there. I can only imagine how hard it is for you."

Fleur nodded, not trusting her voice to speak with all the emotions welling up in her throat. Their grandmother had been more like a mom to her in the years when Fleur's mother had been recovering from the divorce and the depressive spiral that followed it. Jennifer Barclay had mustered energy to fight her husband in court at every juncture of their divorce proceedings, but once she'd won decisive judgments against him and the marriage was truly over, she seemed to lose all sense of purpose.

Lark had been a rock for their mom, ensuring she got the care she needed during those years. Jessamyn had moved in with their father, convinced their mom had persecuted Mateo Barclay unfairly. Their dad had cut off all contact and financial support to both Lark and Fleur as a result. That hadn't stopped Fleur from trying to mend things between them all over the years, but the more she tried to open a dialogue, the more she seemed to alienate everyone. After her breakup with Colin Alexander, she'd given up her peacekeeping efforts. But she still missed her family.

"I wish I'd been here more this past year," Fleur admitted, guilt piling on her shoulders. She'd been so focused on her job, saving up for her own establishment while trying to make a name for herself in the Dallas restaurant community.

She never wanted to be reliant on someone else's support again. She'd turned to Colin at a low point in her life, thinking he'd be a friend and partner. But their relationship hadn't been strong enough to withstand Drake's scorn. He was used to having women fall over him for his good looks and wealth, so maybe it was easy for him to think that's all she'd seen in Colin, too.

"So do I." Lark dropped to sit on a low leather hassock. A bright, inspirational painting of a rainbow over a green field spread out in the background behind her, at odds with her sister's sad expression. "I'll never forgive myself for avoiding Catamount these past few years because of Gibson. I missed out on that time with Gran."

Her sister drew in a slow, shaky breath while Fleur searched for the rights words to console her. Before she could come up with anything, Lark spoke again.

"I was surprised to hear from Drake Alexander this week," she blurted as she stood again, hitching her duffel over her shoulder as if ready to leave the office soon.

"Excuse me?" Straightening, Fleur dragged the tablet closer to her so fast she knocked it sideways on the stand. "What did Drake want?"

"He was feeling me out about making an offer on Crooked Elm."

"What do you mean?" Fleur frowned, wondering why he had said nothing to her about it when he'd known she was the Barclay in residence.

Agitation quickened her pulse.

"He's interested in buying it. I think he hopes we'll sell directly to him without putting it on the market, but I think we should at least wait and see what kind of interest we get first." Lark dug in her bag and came up with a set of keys. "But I need to get to an appointment with a client's school counselor. Message me if you need help with Gran's service."

"I will. And thank you." Fleur nodded absently, still thinking about Drake approaching her sister. She disconnected the call, her tablet going dark before she left the kitchen to wander into the overgrown backyard.

Of course Drake would go behind her back to talk to Lark. But at least the anger chased away the melancholy she'd been feeling. Drake's underhanded tactics let her channel grief and mourning into frustrated outrage.

The rat bastard.

She kept to the flagstone path to avoid tall weeds around the small courtyard where Gran had surrounded a birdbath with perennials, thinking about the awkward conversation she'd had with Drake in the Cowboy Kitchen parking lot. It made a new kind of sense now. She'd been confused that he followed her outside and took the initiative to offer his condolences.

Hell, he'd offered her *a job.*

But all that time he'd simply been gauging her potential willingness to sell him her grandmother's land.

Bending to right the birdbath that had toppled sideways into the lavender and salvia, Fleur vowed not to accept any offer her nemesis made for Crooked

Elm. He couldn't just avoid her because he'd made an enemy out of her.

He'd always thought the worst of her, even before the fiasco of her engagement to his brother. Those years when she'd been travelling to pageants in an effort to win the scholarship prizes, Drake had always been close by to chastise her about her outfits, about the company she kept, about the choices she'd made, nominating himself as a reluctant protector since they were both from the same town. But she hadn't asked for his help. And no matter how well-meaning it might have been at one time, it always came off as judgy. Superior.

But she never could have predicted the level of animosity he'd aimed her way once she got engaged to his brother. He'd been determined to convince her to end things with Colin, and she'd been so upset about how her motives had been misperceived that she'd done exactly that.

Of course, by that time, she'd miscarried, eliminating the secret reason for the engagement in the first place. Under the circumstances, she hadn't had the emotional resources to stand up to Drake and tell him exactly what she thought of his interference, so she'd simply given Colin back his ring.

Setting him free from a commitment he'd only made to her for the baby's sake. But she'd underestimated how devastated she would be—emotionally, physically and mentally—in the aftermath. She'd regretted sending Colin away when she'd needed someone to grieve with her.

But her anger had never been directed toward him, even though he hadn't looked back once he'd left town. No. Her animosity had always been reserved for the man who'd told her she had no business marrying his brother in the first place.

Now, suddenly, Drake needed a favor from her. Well she wouldn't be swayed by his offering her a much-needed paycheck, or pretending to have cared about her grandmother.

Fleur brushed some dirt away from the design molded inside the bowl of the birdbath. Her fingers traced the lines of a sun with a smiling face. She needed to see the Crooked Elm house and grounds shine again even though she couldn't afford to keep the lands. She didn't have money to invest in the work, but she had time and sweat equity. Somehow, she'd find a job to pay her bills.

And just maybe, in the process, she'd figure out a way to heal her broken family, too.

But one thing was certain. She was done needing anything an Alexander man had to offer, ever again.

The scent of lilies and roses hanging thick in the air, Drake noted that the lack of receiving line following Antonia Barclay's memorial spoke volumes about the broken family dynamic.

His gaze swept over the crowd inside the rented hall behind the biggest church in Catamount, seeking the various Barclay sisters since they hadn't even sat together during the memorial. Now that the formal part of the service had finished, the women had dispersed to the opposite corners of the building as they prepared for a meal. And maybe, for his purposes, it was just as well that the siblings didn't have strong family bonds. He wasn't sure how Fleur would feel about him approaching Lark regarding the sale of Crooked Elm. But after the way she'd refused his job offer and reminded him she wouldn't ever trust him again, he'd figured he'd have a better chance of Lark hearing him out.

Too bad she'd seemed distracted when he'd phoned her the week before, telling him she had no plans to return to Catamount beyond the day of the memorial. Which meant this might be his only chance to reach out to the sisters in person.

He tugged his Stetson off his head before heading toward the buffet tables where he'd spied the glint of Fleur's distinctive copper-colored hair a moment before. It didn't make sense that his boots were walking in her direction when they didn't get along. Maybe his conscience hadn't rested easy after their last conversation. There was no love lost between them, but he knew the service had to have been difficult for her. She'd spoken only briefly, her words steady and well chosen, but the dark shadows under her eyes told the toll it had taken.

"Excuse me."

Her voice sounded suddenly behind him, and he turned to see Fleur. He hated the way his blood heated and pulse raced around her, but couldn't pull his gaze away. She wore a simple gray dress dotted with white flowers, understated but not somber.

The hem fell just above her knees, and despite the occasion, he might have still been momentarily distracted by her legs if she hadn't been juggling two large trays. The salvers were heaped with a variety of the Spanish tapas that he recalled Antonia Barclay bringing to community potluck events—savory *croquetas*, some kind of fried potato dish, chorizo and cheeses.

"Whoa. Let me give you a hand." He reached for one of the trays to help, his fingers brushing hers briefly. The contact zinged through him while he turned back to make more room for the food on the closest buffet table. "Shouldn't the catering staff be giving you a hand with this?"

He settled the food between a chafing dish of skewers threaded with chicken and red peppers, and a warming tray full of something that looked like bruschetta, but he was guessing had a Spanish flair. Even the musician in the far corner of the hall played Spanish classical guitar, the whole event themed to showcase Antonia's heritage.

"I must have left my staff in Texas," Fleur snapped while she slid her platter into place near a carafe of red wine. "Along with my job. So I guess I'll just power through on my own."

Confused, Drake stared at all the dishes piled on the buffet tables. There was enough to feed the entire town, the scents of grilled meats and spices wafting through the building while more guests filled the room. The conversation level had increased in volume since the end of the memorial.

"Then who provided all the food?" He couldn't resist swiping one of the *croquetas* from the table, a dish he recalled with fondness.

"Surely not the shallow rodeo pageant queen who saved every cent to attend culinary school." She glared up at him, her eyebrows furrowed as she frowned. "How's the *croqueta*, by the way?"

Surprise made him gulp the food down too soon, but it didn't detract from the taste. Fleur Barclay might be an opportunist, but she was clearly an accomplished chef. And why was it bitter to learn that she had more determination and drive than he'd given her credit for?

"As good as Antonia's," he admitted.

Her expression softened, and the look in her eyes stirred the old heat inside him. A heat he couldn't afford to feel around his brother's former fiancée. That had to be the reason he found himself saying, "And I'll bet attending culinary school turned out to be more rewarding than sacrificing your dreams for marriage, didn't it?"

Her lips flattened into a thin line. Her gray eyes narrowed.

"I don't know about that. I missed out on having you for a brother-in-law, Drake." She folded her arms, her gaze boring into his. "Think about all the fun we could have had silently seething at each other across your family living room every holiday."

The thought of being related to her sent a chill through him, actually. And it wasn't one bit like the charged sensation he'd experienced when their hands had touched. Whatever it was she made him feel, it wasn't an appropriate response to a woman Colin had loved.

"Or not so silently," he amended, hating the vision of Fleur in his brother's arms. "You always enjoyed getting a reaction by needling me."

He should have ignored her when their time on the rodeo circuit had overlapped—him as a bull rider in his twenties, and her showing up to pageants at fairs all over the West in her late teens. But she made it impossible when she constantly drew attention to herself, traipsing through the rodeo grounds in gowns and spangles, attracting all the wrong kinds of attention from guys who didn't know how young she was. Or did, but didn't care, which ticked him off even more. He'd come to her defense more times than she knew, but she'd never made it easy.

Drake might not have been born into the school of hard knocks like Fleur had been, but life had pulled the rug out from under him at eighteen when his parents had died in a freak accident on their property just at the time he was supposed to head to college. An old barn had collapsed, a structure they'd hoped to salvage as part of their lifelong efforts to be good stewards of the land. They had been passionately devoted to conservancy, from local wetlands to limiting their carbon footprint, and they'd tried to save an old barn his mother had found "charming" even though it had an unstable stone foundation.

The day the building caved in devastated the family for years afterward. Drake had sacrificed his own rodeo dreams, keeping one foot on the circuit strictly for the extra earnings while he learned the ranching business for himself. Plus, the bull riding competitions had been flexible enough that he could be home with his younger brother and sister until they finished high school.

But no number of obstacles could have made him turn to using other people to get ahead, the way Fleur had with her engagement to Colin. They'd only dated a few weeks before Fleur had a ring on her finger and the promise of Colin's financial help even if things went south between them.

Why else would Fleur have suddenly decided to sacrifice culinary school to marry Colin instead?

"Good point." Fleur lowered her voice as a couple of older women moved past them to admire the buffet displays. Then, once they'd moved out of earshot, she leaned closer to him. "I could hardly stay silent when you're the type of man to go behind people's backs to get his own way."

The venom behind the words shouldn't surprise him when they'd never been friends. But then, maybe he'd fooled himself thinking she'd ultimately be glad to sell off Crooked Elm.

"I suppose you're referring to me contacting Lark?" He peered around the rented hall again, looking for Fleur's sisters in the crowd.

He needed someone on his side for this conversation since the glint in Fleur's eyes concerned him. If she refused to sell him the ranch, would her siblings be able to override her? He couldn't see either Jessamyn or Lark in the sea of Catamount locals come to say goodbye to the well-liked Barclay widow.

"Of course I am." She tilted her chin at him. "You could have just told me what you wanted that day at the Cowboy Kitchen. Instead you tried to do me a great favor by giving me a job. Was that to make me so grateful I'd sign over Crooked Elm for a song?"

"I'm prepared to make a competitive offer, Fleur," he clarified, wondering if that fact had gotten lost somehow. "I thought it might save you time and trouble for me to take the ranch off your hands—"

"Off my hands?" Her voice rose, breasts rising and falling faster with every agitated breath. "As if it was a burden to spend time in the only place I've ever felt at home in the last sixteen years. Maybe I won't sell a single acre of it until I'm good and ready."

Her eyes shone with emotion as she spoke, and Drake had no doubt that she'd regretted letting him see those feelings by the way she bit down hard on her lower lip afterward.

She spun away from him before he could frame a response, and as much as he would have liked to have continued the conversation and clarify his intentions, he knew her grandmother's memorial was hardly the place. He barely had time to process the conversation when a heavy hand clapped him on the shoulder.

"What's this I hear about selling acres?" a too-jovial male voice asked.

Turning, Drake met the sharp, dark eyes of Mateo Barclay, Fleur's father. Antonia's only son wore a custom-tailored suit and Italian loafers in a crowd full of cowboy boots. His middle daughter, Jessamyn, stood beside him, dressed in a black jacket and matching pencil skirt, her dark wavy hair pinned high on her head. Drake had heard she'd spent the last six years working for her father's real estate development company in Manhattan.

"Hello, Mr. Barclay. I'm so sorry for your loss." Drake shook the other man's hand before offering condolences to Jessamyn.

"So did I hear correctly that you're interested in purchasing my mother's run-down ranch?" Mateo pressed, looking around the crowd as he spoke, as if already searching for someone more worthy of his conversation. He jingled his keys in his pocket and rocked on his heels while he spoke.

It irritated Drake that the guy would bad-mouth the property Fleur had just gotten done saying she loved. Not that he was suddenly on Fleur's side. But her father had struck him as a self-centered blowhard even before his behavior during the divorce.

"I'll be submitting an offer on it soon, yes." Drake wondered why Antonia hadn't given the property to her son but her granddaughters.

"More power to you," Mateo said conspiratorially. "I wouldn't touch the place. Property values out here haven't kept pace with land in vacation destination cities. I tried my best to convince Mom to come to New York, but she was set in her ways." He shook his head before turning to Jessamyn. "Well, I'd say we've put in enough time here. Are you ready to head out?"

"Dad, please," Jessamyn protested quietly. "We haven't even eaten."

"I'll leave you to your dinner, then," Drake said, excusing himself. He nodded to them both, very ready to part ways with Mateo. "Jessamyn, I'll cc you on the offer I make on Crooked Elm. Fleur told me the three of you need to agree when you're ready to sell."

He would have liked to explain his hopes for Crooked Elm, but this wasn't the time.

"Of course." She smiled warmly and passed him her card. "I'll look forward to hearing from you." And then she disappeared into the crowd with her father.

Stuffing the contact information in his jacket pocket, he headed toward the food tables, considering his next move with the Barclay family. He needed their property to continue his parents' legacy of conservation and land restoration efforts. Drake invested heavily in carrying out their work as a way to honor their memory, but he couldn't fulfill his goals in his own backyard while the Crooked Elm continued to be misused by the Barclay family's tenant. He'd tried more than once to convince Antonia Barclay to rent the rangelands to him instead, but she'd refused, insisting that her tenant was working on an irrigation system for the property as part of his reduced rent. Drake had seen little evidence of any such progress. As it stood, a creek that fed the White River wound through his property and the Barclays' ranch lands, and there was no way to restore the wetlands surrounding it without managing the nearby property.

All the ranch lands would be more valuable once he'd restored it. But better for him if Mateo Barclay—the real estate developer—kept thinking Crooked Elm was worthless. Drake didn't need him getting involved in the sale. He'd give Jessamyn a call during the week so they could speak privately.

For now, he'd wait until the meal was over to seek out Fleur again. Not to talk about the deal. Just to smooth things over from earlier. If she was going to spend some time in Catamount enjoying her grandmother's ranch, at least that would mean Drake had more time to convince her to sell to him.

His first step? Making a few fresh memories with her so she could replace the old ones from the day when he'd decimated her hopes of marriage to his brother.

Three

Two hours after she'd served the food, Fleur eyed the buffet tables through the thinning crowd at her grandmother's memorial and decided she could begin cleaning up. Although the preparation for the meal had been a lot of work, she was grateful for the activity on a difficult day. Her grief was too deep to share with the others gathered for the celebration of Antonia's life, so it was better to stay busy now and process the loss later, when the hurt wasn't so fresh.

Excusing herself from a conversation with the local grocer, who'd been sharing a memory of Antonia's early attempts to order fresh octopus when she'd first moved to Colorado, Fleur wove through the people milling around the exit ready to leave. She'd almost reached the buffet when a tall, blonde beauty with hazel eyes approached her, a navy blue dress hugging her slim figure. It took her a moment to recognize Drake and Colin's younger sister, Emma Alexander.

Trepidation seized her even though they'd been friends once. She hadn't seen or spoken to Emma since Fleur had broken off her engagement to Colin.

"Fleur." Emma held her arms wide before wrapping her in a hug scented with the same perfume she'd always worn—something warm and spicy, with a hint of rose. Then, pulling back, she frowned. "I'm sorry about your grandmother. I was late to arrive since I was in Denver getting a last fitting on my wedding dress today, but I wanted you to know how much I loved Antonia. Colin's still living in Montana now, but I'm sure he'd also send his sympathies."

Her chest eased at the kind words and the woman's obvious sincerity. She was glad that Drake's disdain hadn't tainted Emma's view of her. Or if it had, the woman was too well-mannered to show it.

"Thank you so much. And congratulations on your wedding. I didn't know you were engaged." As soon as the words left her mouth, she worried they would call to mind her own failed relationship with Colin, but Emma only beamed.

Fleur could see a resemblance to her oldest brother around the eyes. But where Drake looked at her with dark cynicism, his sister seemed determined to see the good in people. For a moment, it occurred to her that Emma might have that ability because Drake had set aside his own dreams, sacrificing college and the rodeo to ensure his siblings could grow up in their childhood home. But she dismissed the idea again, not sure why her brain wanted to defend Drake Alexander.

"We've been engaged since last Christmas. Glen and I just moved up the wedding to the Fourth of July because we can't wait any longer to start our happily-ever-after." Her smile was infectious, her cheeks glowing pink.

"That's just a few weeks away. Will you have the ceremony locally?" Fleur thought to her own brief engagement. There'd been no thought of wedding dresses then.

There hadn't been time before things fell apart.

"Drake has said we can marry at the ranch, which will be perfect as it can be difficult to change the date with a big venue. But I've been in complete despair about finding anyone to cater it on short notice after the first company I contracted with went out of business suddenly." Emma gave her a sly smile. "Or at least, I despaired about it until today."

Emma pivoted on her nude pumps and gestured toward the buffet tables.

"What?" Confused, Fleur tried to follow her meaning. "I didn't have it catered, so I don't have a name to give you."

"Because you're a chef now!" the other woman said enthusiastically. "Just like you always wanted to be. And you fed half the town today on your own. Wouldn't you consider doing the same thing for my wedding? I have a very generous budget, too, but it's been impossible to find someone good to make the trip all the way out to Catamount, especially on short notice."

The request was so flattering, so exciting, she reeled. Still, even if she could pull off something like that, she wasn't sure it would be a good idea. She had no desire to see Colin again after the way they'd parted, and spending time around Drake—who'd never liked her—was surely an even worse idea.

"Oh no, Emma. I can't do a formal, sit-down meal or anything. I just thought this would be a nice way to remember Antonia—"

"Of course, this was perfect." Emma squeezed her arm gently. "You served all the things we remember her cooking. And that's why I'd love the same foods at my wedding. Antonia brought meals to my family for weeks after my parents died. She was so good to us. To me, in particular."

Emma was only ten at the time of her parents' deaths. Fleur remembered that awful summer when the barn had caved in with the Alexanders inside. She'd heard reports afterward that Mrs. Alexander had been pinned under debris and her husband had gone in to help, but then the rest of the structure fell, killing them both. She'd been one year older than Emma and had grown tongue-tied around the neighbor who'd been through something so traumatic.

"I hadn't realized," Fleur mused, touched anew by her grandmother's generous heart. She would have had her hands full keeping track of Fleur for months on end, yet she'd made time to extend herself to a motherless child, too. "Can I have a few days to think about it and get back to you next week?"

She hadn't secured a job yet, so the income would be welcome. But would the work put her too much in the path of Drake and Colin? She wasn't ready to face either of them anytime soon.

Then, as if called by her thoughts, she met Drake's dark-eyed stare from across the room. A buzz of awareness zipped through her, her nerve endings humming to life. No doubt that only happened because he made her wary. She needed to be on guard around this charismatic—ruthless—man. And yet, she couldn't deny the prickly sense of something… *more* between them.

"Certainly. And I'm sorry if this wasn't a good time to bring it up." The younger woman frowned.

She tore her attention from Drake, wondering if her attention had been obvious. Her cheeks warmed. "I'm glad we talked about the wedding. I'm thrilled for you, Emma."

"Can I help you with the cleanup?" she offered.

"No, thank you. I saw Lark head into the kitchen a few minutes ago. She'll help." Maybe. Her sisters had sat far from one another during the meal. *Would they avoid her in an effort to avoid each other?*

How would they ever agree on what to do with Crooked Elm and the rest of their grandmother's possessions if they never spoke to one another?

Once Emma left, Fleur busied herself with collecting empty trays and condensing leftovers onto a couple of plates. Then she backed through the swinging door into the kitchen, where Lark was already at the industrial-sized sink doing dishes, a borrowed canvas apron wrapped around her simple black sheath dress. But then Lark had never put much stock in appearances. Fleur's brainy sister believed in getting the job done, and had zero patience for fools. Hot water steamed around her while she scoured a chafing dish.

A rush of love for her sister soothed some of the hurts of the day.

"Thank you so much—" Fleur began.

"No need for thanks. If I didn't have a task to occupy my hands, I would have strangled our father. Jessamyn practically had to duct tape him into his chair to get him to stay at his own mother's memorial." Lark used her wrist to shove a hank of limp hair off her forehead.

Fleur scraped dishes and stacked them, choosing her words carefully since their father's favored daughter had frequently been a sore subject for Lark. For that matter, their father was an even sorer subject. "You know how differently people cope with grief. Dad's never done well with deep emotions."

Her sister made a derisive noise. "Right. Like love for his own daughters. Tough stuff."

Before Fleur could answer, the swinging door pushed open again, emitting a brief rush of conversation and Spanish guitar music. Jessamyn strode purposefully into the kitchen, balancing a tray stacked with glassware.

She looked so put together wearing her sleek designer watch, red-bottom heels and tailored suit.

Jess's hair was the same shade as Lark's, but where Lark's had never known a curl, Jessamyn's waves were the stuff of shampoo commercials. Today she wore it tamed into an updo, where it was efficient and beautiful. Yet Fleur always liked seeing it twisted around her sister's shoulders like a living thing.

"The food was incredible, Fleur," Jessamyn announced as she settled the precarious load onto an empty spot. "I held it together through the whole service, but then one taste of the tortilla Española and I was overcome with nostalgia. It tasted exactly like Gran's."

Fleur's throat closed up at the compliment, especially from Jessamyn, who prided herself on not displaying messy emotions. Fleur had held it together all day, too, but the reminder of why she'd worked so hard to feed everyone threatened to unleash the grief she'd tucked away for later.

She glanced between Lark, the brainiac therapist, and Jessamyn, the corporate shark, and wished they could share their hurts more often.

"Thank you. It was weirdly comforting to cook in her kitchen. I thought it would be hard, and in some ways it was. But eventually, it felt peaceful, like I truly would always have a part of her with me." She blinked to keep the emotions at bay and noticed Lark had shut off the faucet to join them. "It almost seemed like she wanted me there."

"Oh, hon. Of course she did," Lark rushed to assure her, sliding an arm around her shoulders while Jessamyn reached to take her hand.

How sad that it took a loss in their family to bring them all together. Standing shoulder-to-shoulder with them reminded her of how many years they'd spent happily under one roof, doing all the things sisters take for granted when they're young. Braiding one another's hair. Sharing toys and books. Sleeping lumped in the same bed during thunderstorms.

Or later when their parents fought, and the sound of angry voices vibrated through the walls.

She could sense the instant her sisters began to retreat. Unwilling for the moment to end, she squeezed Jessamyn's hand tighter and clapped the other on top of Lark's so she couldn't let her go.

"Wait. I know you both have to leave tonight, but I want you to come back to the ranch this summer before we sell the place." She hadn't known she was going to ask it until the words left her mouth. Yes, she needed the money from the sale. But somehow she knew she couldn't allow her finances to dictate what happened next with Crooked Elm.

"Fleur, my work keeps me so busy," Jessamyn started while Lark protested, "I don't know how I can get the time off—"

"Please. Just think about trying to make it happen. If the ranch is our only shared legacy, then we should *share* it. However briefly." She eased her grip on her siblings' hands, understanding they needed to decide for themselves whether or not they would return.

But in the end, they both nodded.

"I'll try," Lark promised.

"Me, too," Jessamyn echoed, backing away. "But

I should go. Dad and I are flying to New York to-night. We need to get on our way."

Fleur breathed easier, having secured that much from her sisters.

"Thank you for keeping him here this long," Fleur called after her while Lark remained silent beside her.

Jessamyn waved an acknowledgment as she sailed out the swinging door. Lark returned to the dishes, shoving up her sleeves and cranking on the faucet.

They were a long way from the sisters they'd been once. And maybe they'd never have that kind of love for one another again. But Fleur thought maybe one day, there was still a chance they could be a family.

Seated on his truck tailgate outside the town's rec center, Drake had started to wonder if Fleur had gone home with someone else. A thought that irri-tated him a lot more than it should.

The parking area was empty of every vehicle save hers. He'd moved his truck to the spot beside her and waited, needing to speak to her again. To clarify his intentions where Crooked Elm was concerned and make peace with her.

Especially now that Emma had approached Fleur about possibly catering her wedding. He'd been sur-prised by that news, considering how picky his sister had been about all the arrangements for her nuptials. Fleur might be an excellent cook, but she wasn't a caterer. He just hoped like hell she didn't refuse Emma because of her feelings about him. God knew, the woman could be prickly. He didn't want his sister hurt.

A moment later, a shaft of light spilled out onto the parking lot where the back door of the rec center opened. Fleur emerged, her hair now in a high ponytail as she balanced two large sacks on one arm and carried an open box in the other.

Drake shoved to his feet and jogged toward her. He'd gone home an hour ago to change into a pair of jeans and T-shirt, while Fleur was still in her gray wrap dress, the fabric hugging her curves in a way he sure as hell shouldn't be noticing.

"Let me help." He took the heavy box from her as soon as he reached her. "Is your car open?"

"No. My keys are in my bag. But what are you still doing here?" Her gaze drifted over him.

She was probably just noting the change of clothes. Still, he liked having her eyes on his body.

And damn it, but he needed to resolve the business between them so he could stay away from her. Bad enough to be attracted to his brother's former fiancée. But when it was also the woman he'd steered his sibling away from, the attraction felt all the more wrong.

"Once again, I find myself wanting to correct a bad impression I made on you when we spoke earlier." He set the box on the ground beside the trunk of her car before taking the sacks she carried out of her arms so she could find her keys.

Fleur nodded as she riffled through her bag. "Because you want to buy the land. Otherwise, you'd never dream of being nice to me."

She withdrew a small key ring with a silver medallion of a running horse from her purse. Inserting the key into the lock, her trunk lifted, albeit with a creaking protest.

"That's not entirely true." He settled the box inside the trunk next to a tire iron. "I've dreamed of being nice to you before." He hadn't meant to drop his tone an octave, but there was no help for it now. "What I mean is—it's not hard for me to be civil."

He busied himself with the other two bags, stowing them away.

"Fine. I'm all ears for this effort you're making to be…less wretched than I remember." She leaned a hip on the bumper of her car and tilted her head to one side to observe him.

Her ponytail slid off her shoulder, exposing an expanse of pale skin at her neck.

He battled the urge to shut his eyes and pinch the bridge of his nose to will away visions of tasting her there.

"Will you sit with me for a minute?" Shutting the trunk of her car, he gestured toward the open tailgate of his pickup, silver metallic paint gleaming in the moonlight. "It's a beautiful night."

Nodding, she straightened and walked closer. He fisted his hands to keep from offering her a boost, but he couldn't stop his gaze from going to the indent at her waist, where it would have been easy to lift her.

Once she'd hoisted herself up, he did the same. A

barn owl screeched from somewhere nearby, filling the air with the unholy call.

"A beautiful night for alien invaders, maybe," Fleur muttered, wrapping her arms around herself. "What *is* that godawful sound?"

He laughed, grateful for a momentary reprieve from hammering out some kind of accord between them.

"That's a barn owl, city girl. You've been gone a long time."

She shivered. "Well, it's spooky enough to be a sound effect in a horror film."

"Have you been in Dallas this whole time?" He recalled that's where her family used to live when they first started coming to Catamount in the summers, before the divorce that catapulted the members to opposite coasts.

"Yes. I gravitated there after things went south with Colin. My mom is on the West Coast near Lark, and my father's business is based in New York, so that's where Jessamyn lives."

He wanted to ask why she hadn't gone to either of those places after her engagement ended, but he knew it was none of his business when he'd been the cause of the split. Or maybe he just didn't want to stir up bad memories.

"I noticed your father kept his distance today," he observed instead. "Lark still doesn't speak to him, either?"

She shook her head. "No. I, on the other hand, will always speak to him, but he makes sure we're never close enough for that to happen. Lark says he's prone to obsessive rumination, and he also has high anxiety levels, but I think he's just an excellent grudge holder."

The pale ribbon that tied her wrap dress fluttered in the breeze, and she captured it between her thumb and forefinger, smoothing them down the silky length.

"Tough to imagine anyone Antonia parented being so tightly wound." His gaze strayed to her calves where her legs swung off the tailgate. When he caught himself, he whipped his attention back to her face, cursing the wayward chemistry. "But I wanted to talk to you tonight so that you'd know my offer to buy Crooked Elm is both sincere and reflective of fair market value."

Her lips flattened into a frown. "It's not even on the market yet, and I haven't had time to research comparable properties."

"I assure you, I have researched it—"

She swung on him with a huff of indignation. "You can't believe I'd take your word for what's an appropriate figure given our relationship."

Something in her tone got under his skin.

"We don't have a relationship." He let the words linger a moment, giving them weight. "But I tried to be a good neighbor to Antonia, and I'd like to think she appreciated my efforts."

"Then why didn't you convince *her* to sell if you were on such great terms?" Her raised voice told Drake how far off track the conversation had gotten.

Hadn't he been trying to smooth things over with her? Wrestling down his annoyance, he explained, "I believe she would have sold to me if she hadn't been committed to giving her granddaughters the option of keeping the place if they chose. But from what I can see, it doesn't look like any of you want to make a life here."

"How would you know what I want?" She tipped her head up to look at the stars. "You don't understand the first thing about me."

"You haven't set foot in Catamount for five years. Not even for Antonia. Are you trying to tell me you suddenly want to be my neighbor?"

"I haven't been here because of *you*," she shot back, sliding off the truck bed and landing on her feet. "You did nothing to hide your distaste for me, and did everything you could to ruin my relationship with Colin. Especially when I needed his support. Do you have any idea how much I dreaded returning to this town with you in it?"

Seeing her this agitated—this hurt and furious—raked over his conscience for a moment. She hadn't let him glimpse those emotions five years ago. He'd been surprised, in fact, that she'd backed down about her engagement to his brother. He'd expected a battle from her, or at least some passionate defense of her love for his brother when Drake had lobbied for her to rethink marriage. Instead, she'd acquiesced.

Now, he latched on to her words. "What do you mean that you needed his support?" He'd thought she needed Colin's money. "Financially?"

An angry sound erupted from her throat before she pivoted on her heel and marched toward the driver's side of her car.

"Fleur?" He hopped off the tailgate to follow her, wondering what he'd missed. "Explain it to me. If you didn't mean money, what did you need from Colin?"

She spun around so fast the hem of her dress whipped at his legs and he had to stop short not to run into her.

"You know what, Drake? I don't owe you any explanations. I didn't then, and I don't now." She was so close he caught a hint of her perfume, vanilla and nutty. Her breath brushed his cheek. "For that matter, you're the last man on earth I'd take a cent from, so I won't be selling Crooked Elm to you."

Her warmth and scent so close to him distracted him from understanding her words for a fraction of a second. So by the time he'd processed the blow she'd just dealt, she was already sliding into the driver's seat.

"Fleur, wait." He'd screwed this up. Badly. And with the land at stake, he couldn't afford to make things personal with Fleur. "Don't make a decision now, while you're upset."

"Good night, Drake." She reached for the car door to pull it closed, then hesitated, glancing up at him. "And I'm not going to be the one to tell Emma you blew her chances of having me cater her wedding. That's on you for always assuming the worst of me.

But then you don't have a great track record when it comes to talking to your siblings."

He would have argued, but since she shut the door, he thought it better to get his feet out of the way of her tires as she put the vehicle into reverse.

How could he lose the land he needed *and* mess up his sister's wedding plans at the same time? Yet he found it tough to ruminate on those things when Fleur's words still echoed in his mind about needing Colin's support. Had there been more to his brother's engagement than he'd known at the time?

Fleur's engine revved as she pulled onto the county road, and he realized he felt uneasy about how upset she'd been. Her anger had seemed genuine enough, making him question everything he'd thought he'd known about her in the past. All he'd known was that his brother went from an easygoing fellow when he started dating Fleur, to a tense, sadder man when they got engaged. He'd refused to talk about his relationship with Fleur, and once they'd broken up, Colin had hightailed it out of town. They'd barely spoken since.

He slammed the tailgate closed on his truck, listening to the barn owl still complaining overhead. Maybe Fleur was just a good actress, and her outrage had been for show. But if it wasn't—if Drake had missed something about his brother's rush to wed—then he needed to figure out what had happened. And since Fleur made it clear she wouldn't be giving him any explanations, that meant he'd need to give his brother a call.

Drumming his fingers on the cool metal of the truck fender, Drake suspected he should feel remorse at the possibility of screwing up Colin's love life five years ago. But with the memory of Fleur's fragrance stirring his senses, he couldn't help thinking it was still just as well that he'd come between them. Because what kind of special torment would it have been to feel like this about his brother's wife?

Four

"Volume up." Fleur gave the voice command to the Bluetooth speaker playing a traditional tango song, an almond scent filling the kitchen.

The lilt of guitars and bandonion had her swaying from the counter to the oven to check on the *polvorones*, almond cookies that her grandmother used to send to her every Christmas. Fleur had found four different recipes for the holiday treat in Antonia's notes, but none of them tasted quite like what she remembered. For the past two days, she'd been winging it, combining elements from the recipes to try to re-create the perfect texture.

After peering through the window into the turquoise oven dating from the seventies, Fleur pulled the door open and withdrew a cookie sheet, setting it on the stove top. A thumping noise made her think for a moment that the bass line in the tango song had sped up. But then she realized someone was knocking at the door.

The outline of a Stetson through the sidelights made her breath catch for a moment. She hadn't seen or heard from Drake since their encounter in the parking lot after her grandmother's memorial, and he'd been in her thoughts far more than he deserved ever since. She regretted losing her temper to the degree that she threatened not to cater Emma's wedding. Not only was it unnecessarily rude to Emma, whom she liked. But it was also cutting off her nose to spite her face since Fleur really needed the paycheck.

And the potential word-of-mouth clients that might come afterward.

An instant later, however, it became apparent from the size of the man's outline that it couldn't be Drake. The newcomer was both shorter and wider than the tall, muscular rancher next door.

Not that she'd given much thought to Drake's body, damn it. She called a voice command to the Bluetooth speaker to lower the volume on her tango music before opening the door.

"Hello. Can I help you?" she greeted the stranger.

A grizzled older man pushed his hat back on his head as he took her measure in the June sunlight. Dirt-smudged overalls suggested he'd been working with his hands.

"I'm not sure. I'm Josiah Cranston, your grandmother's tenant. I've been trying to reach you to find out your plans for Crooked Elm since I've been leasing most of the rangelands for the last five years."

"Fleur Barclay." She extended her hand, remembering the small cottage that had once served as the foreman's quarters for Crooked Elm. Her grandmother had rented out the house when she'd leased the acreage. "Thank you for stopping by. Would you like to come in?"

The man's lower lip curled, hesitating. "I'm not really fit for company since I've been in the fields. I just wanted to see if you're still planning to lease to me this year or if I'll need to make other arrangements?"

His voice was gruff, his tone impatient as he shuffled from foot to foot on the welcome mat.

"I apologize, Mr. Cranston. My sisters and I haven't had the chance to discuss our next move, but we are considering selling the ranch." There was no other way to afford her dream of owning a restaurant. And she understood the financial windfall would help Lark, who'd been struggling to make ends meet since her divorce after refusing her ex-husband's offer of alimony. Fleur understood all too well the need to be independent after the games their father had put them through with finances.

Jessamyn might not need the funds, but she certainly had no sentimental attachment to the Crooked Elm. A fact that struck Fleur as very sad when they'd all been happy here once.

The rancher on the porch narrowed pale blue eyes

at her, then took a moment to spit over one side of the porch rail.

"Well, that's not going to make things easy for me. But that's no concern of yours, I suppose." Another spit. "The creek has been drying up, anyway. I don't think you're going to have much luck selling a property with no irrigation."

She wanted to ask him why he'd want to keep renting the land if it was no good, but his confrontational demeanor kept the thought on lockdown. "I'm surprised to hear about the creek. Maybe it's just a dry year?"

"Nope. Bad land management practices. But your grandma didn't have any money to put into the place." He rocked on his heels, old boots creaking under his weight.

She bristled at the slight.

"What do you mean 'bad land management'? Gran hadn't even ranched the land for over a decade." She should have made it a priority to walk more of the property. Or borrow a horse and ride it so she could see for herself what it looked like these days. Antonia had long ago sold off all but a few goats that she kept for making her own cheeses.

"Why don't you ask your neighbor about that?" he suggested, smiling in a way that looked more like a grimace, showing tobacco-stained teeth. "The Alexander boy is the local conservation hero. I'm sure he'll be too glad to tell you everything your grandmother was doing wrong here dating back to well before my time."

Drake? He was the last person she wanted to talk to these days, but before she could quiz Josiah any more, the man tipped his hat in a way that seemed more than a little patronizing as he wished her a "good day."

She fixed a polite expression on her face and said goodbye, but as soon as she closed the door she asked no one in particular, "How am I supposed to have a good day now?"

Worried, Fleur wandered over to the stove and lifted a spatula to move her *polvorones* to a cooling rack while she considered her next move. She didn't know anything about local conservation efforts or land management practices. Her ranching knowledge was limited to horseback riding, summer vacations at Gran's and whatever she'd learned in 4-H about animals. Oh, and she could make cheese from goat's milk, too. A good thing, since she'd inherited her grandmother's goats and had been caring for them daily.

Had Antonia known the creek was drying up? Or was Josiah just trying to worry Fleur about selling the land so she'd keep leasing it to him? Gran had kept her tenant on because the income paid the yearly land taxes and provided enough for Gran's living expenses. But would she have continued to lease to him if she'd known about the irrigation problems?

She had no way of knowing the answers to those questions, but she suspected Josiah was right that Drake would know. She'd overheard a conversation at the feedstore earlier in the week about how he'd expanded his father's operation and how successful he'd become with his yearling steers. Drake wasn't just playing at being a rancher. He was the real deal.

Maybe it was just as well that she had a reason to visit Alexander Ranch. She owed Emma an answer about her wedding, and if she had to eat humble pie in front of Drake for letting her temper get the better of her, she would do so. Emma had always been kind to her, even in the old pageant days when most of her peers had written her efforts off as attention-seeking.

Still, the thought of seeing Drake again stirred a hunger inside her...

With a curse, she swiped one of the warm cookies off the cooling rack and took a big bite. The rush of sugar and almond was perfect, as was the wave of nostalgia that followed. The crumbly, shortbread-like texture transported her to Christmases past when she would bite into the treats her grandmother shipped to their family. Excited, she knew she'd found the right combination for the recipe and made a note in her food binder.

Even better, she'd have a freshly baked confection to offer in a trade for information at the Alexander Ranch. *Polvorones* beat the taste of humble pie any day. Besides, she seemed to need a substitute snack lately whenever she thought of Drake after their last encounter. She'd never stood so close to him as she had in the parking lot under the stars.

And she recalled the precise moment during her tirade when her anger at him had suddenly felt like something entirely different. Something twitchy and hungry. Like maybe she wanted to throw herself into his arms instead of arguing with him.

Just remembering the moment inspired the need to fan herself. So, as she packed up the cookies in a container to walk over to the ranch next door, she reminded herself that Drake Alexander had assumed the worst about her five years ago, upsetting her so much that she'd done exactly what he'd suggested and broken things off with his brother.

Hurting herself in the process, since it meant losing Colin's support at the most difficult time of her life.

Come to think of it, had her behavior been all that different at the memorial when she'd allowed Drake to rile her so much she threatened not to cater Emma's wedding? Hadn't she learned anything in the last five years? Wasn't she a more responsible, level-headed woman than the one who'd left Catamount back then?

By the time she slipped on her boots and headed out the back door again, Fleur acknowledged that Drake had done her wrong, and she had every right to be angry about that. But she couldn't deny that when she thought about the past, the bigger anger she saved for herself.

With a shift of his knee, Drake nudged Pearl, his paint mare, closer to a feeder creek for the White River. Careful to avoid a patch of new wetland plants, he slowed Pearl's pace so he could withdraw his phone to take some photos of the area. The difference in the plant growth along the creek here, versus farther south after the waterway passed through the Crooked Elm rangelands, was dramatic.

He'd been working with the local conservancy group on better land management practices to bring the wetlands back these past three years. The efforts were time intensive, but the long-term benefits couldn't be overstated. If only Antonia Barclay had agreed.

Because it sure seemed like her stubborn granddaughter would never even hear him out. Too much bad blood for them to hold a civil conversation for more than five minutes. He huffed out a long exhale at the thought of Fleur, wondering if Colin would ever return his calls about her. Taking a gamble, he switched his phone out of camera mode and hit the button to dial his brother's number.

Again.

He'd already left messages. Texted. He hated that his relationship with his younger brother had disintegrated to this point, where they only spoke a couple of times a year. After their falling-out over Fleur, Colin had relocated to Montana, where he'd attended college.

"Drake?" Colin's voice in his ear surprised him after the radio silence this whole week. "Everything okay?"

"Yes, things are fine here." No surprise Colin would worry that something was wrong in the family since Drake hardly ever checked in. "Thanks for picking up. I've been trying to reach you all week."

He heard the judgment in his voice, but it was too late to scrub it out now. He tipped his head to view the cloudless blue sky, breathing in the cooler, pine-scented air blowing off the mountains to the east. This place had a way of calming him down and soothing the raw patches inside. He'd never leave this land that his parents had worked with their own hands, land they'd died trying to better.

"I figured I'd call you on the weekend," Colin muttered, a distant buzz sounding in the background of the call. A tractor, maybe. "We did a big gather this week and needed some outside hands, so I've been overseeing a lot."

Drake understood that moving a big herd over rough range could be time-consuming. He wished—not for the first time—that his brother had bought land closer to home. What was Drake pushing himself for to expand the Alexander Ranch operation if not for the benefit of Alexanders?

But he stuffed down those thoughts to focus on why he'd called. He urged Pearl away from the creek bed to head toward home. "Sorry to pester you. But a question has come up for me this week now that Fleur Barclay is back in Catamount."

The answering silence felt heavy. Hostile?

He hoped not. They hadn't spoken of her in five years. Unbidden, an image of Colin and Fleur laughing together over a basket of puppies flashed through his head. The foreman's Great Pyrenees, Myrtle, had birthed a litter and Colin had invited Fleur over to play with the pups. It had been the first—the only time—he'd seen the two of them together as a couple. The image had burned into him even then.

"Emma told me about Fleur's return," Colin said finally, voice even. If he still had feelings for Fleur, Drake couldn't have guessed it from his tone. "And I was sorry to hear about Antonia's passing." He paused a long moment before continuing. "You mentioned a question?"

"Fleur said something the other night, after her grandmother's memorial, that made me think there was more to your engagement than what you told me." He recalled her expression perfectly, pretty gray eyes full of distress and anger. Her expressive mouth pulled into an unhappy frown.

The split from Colin had upset her deeply. Was it just because they were so in love? The idea bothered him. Made him wonder if he'd read the situation all wrong back then. He'd been so sure they weren't right for each other, even if she *hadn't* been marrying Colin for the payout.

"First of all, my brother, that's not a question." Colin's voice had an edge. "Secondly you'll have to ask her if you want to know more about that subject. And if that's all you needed, I've got a pasture full of protective mama cows and calves that need moving."

"Wait—" Drake had a follow-up question, but his phone screen showed the call had already ended.

He shoved the device into the pocket of his jeans and was about to nudge Pearl faster when movement from a clearing caught his eye. Turning, he spied a distinctly feminine form in a bright red

T-shirt and jean cutoffs heading toward him, a basket over one arm.

Fleur.

Her hair blew around her shoulders, the color more blond than red in the sunlight. And the T-shirt she wore didn't quite reach the waistband of her shorts, a sliver of skin visible as she moved toward him. What was it about that narrow strip of skin that mesmerized him? He wanted to slide his palms around her there, feel that smooth skin against his hands as he crushed her to him.

He could deny wanting her—and he'd tried that, damn it, he'd *tried*—but that had never eased his fascination with this woman. For a moment, he let the truth of that knowledge wash over him, wishing they could have met under different circumstances, without all the baggage of their shared past.

And his brother's old claim on her.

Standing still as she picked her way along the path between the ranches, Drake was grateful for how long it took her to close the distance between them. It took him every second of that time to get command of himself.

"I was on my way to Alexander Ranch to offer an olive branch," she announced once she neared him, her eyes fixed on Pearl and not him. "What a gorgeous horse you have. May I say hello to her?"

Wary of her motive behind a peace offering, Drake still needed to accept it when he had questions for her.

"Of course." He lifted his leg over the mare's back

and slid to the ground. "This is Pearl, daughter to one of my mother's favorite mares, Black Pearl."

He didn't speak of his parents often, but he thought Fleur might recall the animal. And maybe the topic was his own attempt at a truce, reminding her of a time before the animosity between them.

"I remember Black Pearl," she whispered, stroking Pearl's all white nose. "I admired your mother's horsemanship. She always encouraged me in my riding." Her gaze darted toward him, perhaps checking for his reaction to a conversation about his mom.

He realized he wanted to hear what she had to say, however. His own store of memories about his parents was far too limited, and often overshadowed by the argument he'd had with them the last time they'd spoken.

Your siblings look up to you, Drake. You need to set a better example...

"Did she?" Drake prompted her, scratching behind Pearl's ear when Fleur's hand fell away.

She nodded. "I was never as good as Emma because we didn't have horses at our house in Dallas. But your mom always picked out a calm animal for me to ride and gave me new confidence."

Fleur's smile lit her entire face, the memory clearly a good one for her. He couldn't recall ever seeing that happy light in her eyes before. Not even when she'd been engaged to his brother.

The thought gave him pause, as he wondered if life had been tougher for her than he'd realized.

"I'm glad to know that about my mother, although

it doesn't surprise me to hear." Clearing his throat, he put aside his own memories to focus on her. "Were you coming to the house? I'm not sure if Emma's around, but you're…welcome either way."

He couldn't help the halting words. He and Fleur had been opposing forces for too long. And Colin had insisted Fleur was the only one who could fill Drake in on the blanks in his mind about her broken engagement.

"I did plan to bring these to your sister." She lifted a yellow tea towel laid over the willow basket she carried to show him the sweets within. "I wanted to apologize for my hasty words and let her know I would cater her reception if she still has need of my services."

"If I promise I never told Emma otherwise, can I try one of these?" His hand hovered over the cookies as he inhaled the scent of almond and butter.

"They're *polvorones*, and thank you, Drake. Keeping quiet about my mean side in front of your sister deserves a reward. Please take one."

Her soft voice and conciliatory words stirred something inside him, and he shoved it ruthlessly aside to focus on the cookies.

Helping himself, he bit into one. They were delicious, like everything else she made. "Oh wow. You didn't have these at the memorial or I would have remembered."

Another smile from her as she tucked the yellow linen around the baked goods again.

"I've been fine-tuning the recipe all week, and I'm really happy with this version."

"They're amazing. Better than anything we offer at the Cowboy Kitchen." He recalled that she needed a job, a job he hadn't been able to convince her to take at the restaurant he now owned. "You should consider selling them there."

"Really?" Her eyebrows lifted in surprise. "You don't think the cook would be opposed to having baked goods brought in from outside?"

Drake shrugged. "Can't hurt to ask." He polished off the rest before gesturing to Pearl. "And we can ride back to the house." He gestured to his horse.

"Oh, that's okay. I'm fine to walk." Her gaze darted between him and the animal.

Then high splotches of color appeared on her cheeks. That hint of awareness made him all the more determined to convince her.

"This is a day of olive branches, after all," he pressed.

Her gray eyes moved over the horse before darting back to him.

"You trust Pearl with two riders?"

"Yes, and she trusts me." Plus the house was less than a mile away. He wouldn't expect the animal to carry the extra weight for any real distance.

His words seemed to have the desired effect because she stepped closer, passing him the basket so she could mount.

He clipped the basket into a carabiner hook on the saddlebag, then held the reins while Fleur put a boot in the stirrup. She hoisted herself up, smooth and easy, like she belonged on horseback. Of course, despite the hard time he'd given Fleur about being a rodeo pageant queen, they didn't choose just anyone to represent the sport. The best were excellent horsewomen.

"Do you want to be in front?" She sat straight in the middle of the saddle, her legs bare and tanned to the tops of her cowboy boots.

"You take the reins." He already knew she rode well. Hell, his mother had given her a stamp of approval. "I'll ride behind."

Pearl would have headed home now even without a hand on the reins. Besides, Drake couldn't deny the desire to feel Fleur in his arms just this once. He knew her well enough to suspect the truce between them wouldn't last, so this could be the only chance he ever had.

Swinging up behind her, he wrapped an arm around her waist, remembering belatedly about the way her short T-shirt didn't quite meet the top of her cutoffs. His forearm pressed into smooth, bare skin, her belly sucking in on a gasp at the contact.

Same, sweetheart. Same.

He breathed in the vanilla scent of her as her back pressed his chest. Her curvy rump pressed… ah, damn. He had to grind his teeth together to keep from thinking about how *that* felt.

Instead, he nudged Pearl's side gently, glancing down to enjoy the way Fleur's legs looked riding along his jeans. Unable to stop himself, he cupped her hip in his palm, knowing full well this moment would be replayed in his head many, many times after today.

"So you decided you won't mind catering the wedding?" he asked to keep his brain rooted in reality and not the fantasy scenarios spinning through his brain.

Pearl took her time down the path toward the barn, slow and steady. She was a damned good horse to keep Fleur right where Drake wanted her. For now, at least.

"I've always liked your sister." She glanced up at him over her shoulder. "I wasn't sure how she felt about me after Colin and I—er, split up. She was away at college then, and I hesitated to reach out to her."

A bird startled out of the grass nearby with a squawk, and the mare did a double step, jarring the riders a bit. Drake's fingers flexed against Fleur's hip bone, his thumb resting in the curve of her waist.

Making it all the tougher to focus.

"Colin never talked about that to anyone that I know of." He forced his thoughts back to the conversation he'd had with his brother just before Fleur had arrived today. "In fact, I asked him again about the engagement after the conversation you and I had the other night. But he said if I wanted to know more, I'd have to ask you."

He waited, their hips rolling forward in synch as the mare went downhill. Fleur's shoulders tensed, but she never tightened her grip on the reins. A credit to her ability to put the horse first.

"It was kind of Colin to maintain my secret all this time, but maybe it would benefit us all to clear the air," she said finally.

"I don't understand." Frowning, he edged to one side to better gauge her expression.

Fleur turned to meet his gaze briefly, her eyes shining with emotion. "I never wanted anyone to know," she said quietly. "I was pregnant."

Five

The secret had spilled out of her more easily than she would have expected after all these years.

Fleur felt a burden slide from her shoulders. Not because she'd confided in Drake, necessarily. Just that she'd spoken the truth to *someone* at long last. But being on horseback with Drake, not fully facing him, had made it easier to divulge the old secret. Or, if she was totally honest with herself, maybe entrusting him with that closely guarded information had also been a way to distract herself from the hyperawareness she experienced being pressed against his hard, masculine body. Every breath she took was scented with pine and leather overlaid with musk and man.

She felt hot all over. On edge.

So perhaps sharing the angst of her past with Colin was an effort to douse the flames.

"My God, Fleur." Drake's voice sounded rough, as if he had a weight on his chest. "I never guessed. And I can't believe Colin didn't say anything—"

"I swore him to secrecy. I wanted to figure out how to tell my parents and my grandmother first. But we planned on telling your family afterward." She peered up over one shoulder at him as the horse entered a tunnel of tall pine trees. The shade cast Drake's expression in shadow, but she could see the set of his jaw, the flat disapproval of his mouth.

"Still, he should have—" He shook his head, frustration clear as he stopped himself midsentence.

"What? He should have broken a promise to me to confide in you? I didn't want everyone to know we were marrying because of the baby, though they'd all figure it out soon enough." It had taken a while, but she'd forgiven Colin for his eagerness to flee town once she'd given him back his ring. Though she did have some resentment at how easy it had seemed for him to let go. Not just of her, but of the future they'd glimpsed together with their child—however briefly.

"That's not what I was going to say." Still holding her waist, Drake wrenched off his Stetson with his free hand, to rake his wrist along his forehead in an impatient gesture. "He had an obligation to you."

"You didn't think so at the time," she reminded him, taking a little too much pleasure in the outlet of bitterness.

"You're right. Of course." The words were softly

spoken as he replaced his hat on his head. He exhaled a slow breath while his grip shifted on the waistband of her shorts, his thumb grazing the bare skin beneath her cropped top.

An accidental brush. No more.

Yet sensation sizzled through her despite everything.

Her pulse quickened and with it the need to lash out. To distance herself from what she felt around him.

"I'll mark it in my calendar as a first. Catamount's resident bull riding champion and ranching king agrees with me, the outcast rodeo queen." She kept her eye on the trail ahead, grateful to see the massive log-and-stone main house where she could dismount.

Had she really thought for a moment she could make peace with this man? His chest rubbed against her shoulder blades with the movement of the mount, his warmth and strength reminding her how long it had been since she'd been this close to any man. Surely that had to be why she couldn't stop picturing what it would be like to turn in his arms and plaster herself to him. Taste him. Touch him.

Why did she have to feel those things for a man who'd never understood her? A man who'd gone out of his way to make sure she knew he didn't approve of her.

"I'm man enough to admit when I'm wrong." His tone hadn't varied from the earlier gentleness.

Something about that—his kindness in the face of her attempts to restore some enmity—only messed with her head. She resisted the urge to look up and over her shoulder at him. They were so close she could have tipped her neck back and her head would have fit into the notch beneath his jaw.

Swallowing hard, she said nothing and silently willed Pearl to walk faster. The house was less than fifty yards away. Surrounded by aspen trees whispering in the light breeze, the sprawling home had to be well over ten thousand square feet. They approached from the back, where a feeder creek to the White River meandered into a wide bend, giving the wide stone patio an elegant water feature at its base. Adirondack chairs surrounded a stone firepit near the creek on one end of the patio, while a wooden dock thrust into the heart of the waterway at the other.

The creek didn't look dry here, the way Josiah Cranston had suggested. But she *had* noted that the waterway on the Barclay property didn't appear as robust. Still, she could hardly blurt out questions about land management no matter how much she didn't want to talk about the past.

"Fleur?" His voice sounded closer, the words warm against her hair even though he didn't touch her there.

The pine and musk scent of him made her want to breathe deeply. A shiver stole through her, and she closed her eyes briefly to ward away whatever illusion of attraction she was feeling.

"What?" She forced the word from her lips with more harshness than she'd intended.

"May I ask—" He swallowed, a movement she felt as he hesitated. "What became of the child?"

Old pain rose inside her, suddenly as jagged and deep as ever it had been. A sense of loss came with it, the rush of emptiness so poignant her hand went to the flat of her belly.

Right where Drake's forearm rested.

She didn't flinch away from him, though, her fingers landing lightly on his skin as she remembered the baby that wasn't meant to be.

"I miscarried early," she admitted, her eyes hot with unshed tears. "Right after Colin drew up the prenup with generous terms for me in case things didn't work out between us. He'd done it to make me feel more secure about giving marriage a try." She needed to press that point, knowing Drake had been convinced she was only marrying Colin for a payday. "When you asked me to break things off, I was no longer pregnant. That's why I agreed."

Behind her, Drake was utterly still. The horse had halted on the grass close to the patio. Pearl gave a shake of her head as if to ward off an itch, but otherwise, stood patiently as the creek babbled past.

"I'm so damned sorry, Fleur." At some point, Drake had tucked her even closer to him, his brawny arm holding her tighter. His cheek rested against her hair. She could feel his heartbeat against her spine. While she knew she should probably pull away, she couldn't find the will to ignore this comfort that she'd never received for her lost child.

And it did feel like comfort. For a moment, she

breathed it in, allowing herself a moment of healing peace that came from his apology.

From his touch.

A tear plopped from her eye onto his forearm. She stared at the wet drop as it melted into the space between her hand and Drake's skin.

"Thank you. It was a long time ago." It had been a confusing time since she'd been scared about the pregnancy and the ways it would change her life, but she'd never *not* wanted the baby.

At the time, it had felt like one more way she'd been denied a family, something she'd been lacking ever since her parents' marriage had imploded. Until she'd miscarried, she hadn't realized how many hopes she'd already built around the life inside her.

"It was a long time ago, which makes my apology not only inadequate, but also overdue." Drake gave her a slight squeeze before releasing her again.

He swung a leg over Pearl's back to dismount, then held up his hands to help her down. A courtesy she hardly required. But considering she felt a bit unsteady, she didn't protest. And somehow, looking into his brown eyes as he eased her to her feet added to the sparks lighting up her insides.

Unwelcome sparks, damn it.

Just because she'd welcomed his comfort didn't mean she would cave to the new awareness of him that grew every time she saw him.

Stepping out of his arms, she reached to unfasten the carabiner that held the basket of freshly baked cookies she'd brought. Belatedly, she remembered her mission today had nothing to do with anything they'd talked about. How could she speak to Drake about wetlands and land management when her pulse was thrumming and her skin felt too tight because of his touch?

"I can get it," he offered, his fingers brushing against hers as he pinched the heavy clip open.

She opened her mouth to argue—she really needed the barrier of a disagreement right now— but her gaze collided with his again. And it amazed her how much different it felt for him to peer at her with warmth and curiosity instead of cold scorn.

Her throat dried up. She sucked in a fast breath, struggling for equilibrium as they stood side by side, their hands on either end of the basket as he freed it.

His attention lowered to her mouth, as if he'd heard that intake of air and understood what it meant. Her heart rattled her ribs so loudly she wondered if he heard that, too.

Mesmerized, she might have turned toward him a fraction.

Until a feminine voice shouted from the house.

"Fleur, it's you!" Emma called to them, making Fleur leap back a step, her basket in her hands. "Drake Alexander, you'd better be inviting her to dinner."

A sigh of relief—it must be relief and not a twinge of disappointment that the moment had been broken—dispelled the turmoil that had been whipping through her a moment ago. Fleur told herself she'd speak to Drake another time, when she wasn't all twisted around and confused about him. She stretched her lips into a welcoming smile for her friend.

"Emma, I'm so glad to see you."

Agitated, Drake spoke softly to Pearl to lead her to the barn. The mare nickered and followed him, her soft nose pressing into his shoulder every now and again, as if to pick up his pace so she could get to her oats faster.

Fleur had been pregnant with Colin's child.

The news floored him. Maybe he should have guessed as much, considering how fast they'd gotten engaged and how uneasy Colin had seemed. Even Fleur hadn't seemed like an eager bride. Which had made Drake wary of their motivations and love. But a pregnancy had never crossed his mind.

And shouldn't that tell him something about how quick he'd been to draw assumptions about Fleur? He regretted that, if only because his interference could have had devastating consequences for the Alexander family line. Yes, she'd said she'd already miscarried by the time Drake convinced her to break the engagement. But what if she hadn't? Would she have still caved to Drake's insistence they were all wrong for one another?

He would have been responsible for separating Colin from the mother of his child. No wonder his brother didn't speak to him.

Reaching the barn, he clipped Pearl into the cross-ties to groom her before her meal. There were ranch hands nearby if he'd wanted to hand off the task, but the simple ritual of brushing down his horse would be a welcome distraction when his mind was working double time.

Because even if he could set aside the fact that Fleur and Colin had shared a deeper connection than Drake had understood, he couldn't escape the other thing circling around and around his brain. There'd been a breathless, heated moment with her just now when he'd nearly kissed her. He would have sworn—in that instant, at least—that she'd wanted him, too.

He removed the saddle and bridle, returning the pieces to the tack room before he retrieved the brush. The stables were empty with the other horses out to pasture, but an older gelding stood near the open doors to the barn in a shady spot he favored.

"Hello, Pharoah." Drake paused to greet the tall palomino with a scratch along the flank.

While he stood there, one foot in the barn and one foot out, he could look at the main house and see the stone patio where his sister and Fleur now sat in the Adirondack chairs by the creek bend. The willow basket of almond cookies sat on a low wooden table between them along with a clear glass pitcher of lemonade Emma must have brought from the house. From almost two hundred yards away, he couldn't hear them, but he could see Fleur's face in profile well enough, her smile and relaxed posture telling him that Emma had put her at ease.

He felt relieved to know Fleur could put aside their conversation enough to enjoy her time with his sister.

Fleur had been visibly upset talking about the miscarriage. It had surprised him when she'd attempted to downplay his role in breaking up her engagement to Colin by assuring him she'd already miscarried by then. He'd been reeling so much from the news of the pregnancy, she could have delivered a knockout blow if she'd allowed him to think he'd robbed her of the father's support at a critical juncture.

Yet she hadn't. Even though he'd most certainly done so.

On the patio, she turned toward him suddenly, as if she'd felt his regard. Awareness crackled to life, like a flame called from red-hot embers beneath the thinnest veneer of ash.

He nodded to Fleur along with a final pat to Pharoah before returning to the cool shadows inside the barn. Finding a currycomb and brushes for Pearl, he returned to the task of grooming the black-and-white dappled paint.

As he worked over the animal, he contemplated his next move, knowing he needed to be warier around the woman. The old enmity between them was fading. How could it stand based on what he knew now?

He'd done Fleur Barclay wrong.

As he'd told her, he could admit a failure. That wasn't the problem wedged between his shoulder blades. Right now, all he could think of was how she'd fit against him when they rode together. How her breath had quickened when his thumb skimmed the band of bare flesh at her waist. How her gray eyes had turned a molten silver in the protracted moment when he'd thought about kissing her.

That was a far bigger problem than the mistake he made five years ago. Because it meant he wanted the woman his brother had loved.

And if he hoped to repair the damage he'd already done to the relationship with his sibling, he could never, ever act on that.

"Would you like any more chicken?" Emma asked Fleur as they finished their dinner that evening. Her hostess had somehow managed to barbecue in a white denim skirt and blousy orange top without getting a drop of sauce on her outfit. Her pear-shaped solitaire engagement ring glinted as she brandished the platter of poultry. "Or should I bring out the *polvorones* for our dessert?"

The two of them sat on the patio as the sun sank lower on the horizon. Emma had produced salads and fresh bread to go with the chicken for an impromptu meal that had been delicious. It had taken a while for Fleur to relax enough to enjoy herself since she kept thinking Drake would join them.

Indeed, Emma remarked on it more than once that he usually joined her for supper. So perhaps he was staying away from the table because of Fleur. Which was just as well, of course. She preferred it, even. The old way of relating to Drake—ignoring him, hating him—was simpler than whatever had happened between them earlier that afternoon when things had turned unexpectedly heated.

"I couldn't eat another bite of anything, Emma. But thank you. All the food was delicious, and I really enjoyed the meal." Fleur shook out her napkin over the grass closest to the picnic table on the patio, then folded the red-and-white gingham linen to lay beside her empty plate.

She had almost convinced herself that she'd imagined those breathless moments with Drake when the air between them crackled with electricity and she swore he would have kissed her.

They'd never even liked each other.

So clearly, her thinking that she'd almost kissed Drake Alexander was just a fanciful imagining.

Reaching across the wrought-iron table, Emma gave Fleur's forearm a squeeze. "It was my pleasure to cook for you and have some time together. I'm just so thrilled you decided to cater the wedding."

Fleur smiled, gladness stealing through her. After navigating the difficult relationships with her sisters, she often felt gun-shy about female friendships. As a result, she hadn't made those deep bonds that some women form with their friends, and her life was the poorer for it. She hadn't expected Emma to extend her the warmth of friendship so readily after the broken engagement.

The thought brought her former fiancé's face to mind. She really needed to ask Emma an awkward question.

"Erm. One thing about the wedding." She shifted position on the bench, forcing herself to meet Emma's wide hazel eyes. As much as she wanted this job—and she really, really needed the income at this point—she didn't want to create unease in the Alexander family. "You know things ended unhappily between Colin and me. You're not concerned it might be awkward for him? Having me so involved in your big day?"

Emma's head tilted to one side, her lips drawing into a small frown. "I hope it won't be hard for him, but given how little effort he's made to patch things up with Drake since their falling-out over you, I won't let his feelings dictate my choices."

Fleur reared back a bit, trying to get a handle on what she'd just heard. Her bare thighs beneath her cutoffs raked along the wrought-iron seat at the movement.

"They quarreled?" She hadn't known there was tension between them—then or now. "And you think it was over me?"

"You didn't know?" Emma's eyes went round as she shoved aside her plate and leaned her elbows on the table. "When Colin moved to Montana, he intended it as a way to put distance between him and Drake. He hasn't been home since…you know." She looked abashed, her voice dropping. "Things ended with you."

Fleur shook her head, unable to believe that she'd been the cause of that sort of standoff.

"There had to be more to it than me. Colin and I—we weren't meant to be. He knew that as well as I did." She just hadn't always liked to admit that to herself since hanging on to her anger with Drake had been easier than blaming Colin, who'd been her friend before he'd been her lover, however briefly.

She thought back to his brief visit to her at her grandmother's house when she'd told him there was no point in remaining together since she'd miscarried their baby. He'd been kind. Tender, even. And he'd wished her well when she'd given him back his ring.

It would have all been a distant memory for her except that she'd been deep in her own grief. His departure from her life, when she needed someone to grieve with her, or to at least hold her while she cried, had been devastating. Only after he walked out her door for good did she give in to the emotions overwhelming her. She'd cried for days. Weeks, maybe. Time had been a slippery concept in those days of despair and, she realized later, a huge shift in hormones that made it even tougher to get her emotions under control.

Yet she hadn't blamed Colin, choosing to see his brother as the one responsible for pressing her to end the engagement. Now, she had to wonder why she'd been content to paint Drake as the villain in their drama. Why did she reserve all her animosity for him? But then, Drake had always inspired strong emotions in her.

Even now, her thoughts went to him and not to his brother far away in Montana.

"Do you really think so?" Emma mused, toying with the blond ends of her ponytail. Around them, the gas-fueled tiki torches around the patio flamed to life, giving a golden cast to the evening as the sun disappeared behind tall pines. "I'll be honest that I never saw the two of you as the right fit for one another." Her hazel gaze was shrewd for a moment before she smiled. "Either way, if he wanted a say in my wedding planning, he could have come home to congratulate me or visit me anytime in the past five years."

A new uneasiness returned as Fleur considered what she'd learned. There were dynamics at work in the Alexander family she'd been unaware of and felt unprepared to deal with during the catering job. She empathized, having dysfunction galore in her own family, though it made her uncomfortable that she could be the source of Drake and Colin's conflict. But since she wouldn't be able to afford to keep the electric on at the ranch next month if she didn't have some kind of work, she planned to forge ahead anyhow.

She stood to help Emma clear the table, changing the subject to other wedding details in an effort to lighten the mood. But even as Emma described her dress in detail, and explained her plans for exchanging vows beside the creek in her own backyard, Fleur's thoughts kept returning to Drake.

Not just the way he held her on horseback. Or the charged moment when she thought he might have kissed her. She also wondered what had happened between the Drake brothers to make Colin leave Catamount for good.

What if the misunderstanding concerned her, or

was in her power to fix? Fleur knew how much it hurt to have warring siblings.

Making up her mind to talk to Drake about it when she approached him about the land management issue, she said good-night to Emma, knowing she should start the walk home before it got any darker.

The women exchanged a hug.

"Let me give you a ride home," Emma offered.

Fleur shook her head. "That's okay. The fresh air will do me good."

She had too much on her mind, especially that exchange with Drake.

"Then you can take one of the horses," Emma insisted as they stood on the flagstones, the creek rippling at their feet. "It's too far to walk, especially at this hour. And Drake is probably still in the barn. He can saddle one for you."

"I'll be fine," Fleur vowed as she edged onto the damp grass. Because even though she'd decided to speak to Drake, she hadn't quite recovered enough from their last conversation to spend more time with him tonight. "I'll take the path that follows the creek."

"And what if you step into a bog?" Emma argued, distracted by her vibrating phone. She checked it briefly before stuffing the device into her skirt pocket. "A horse will keep you safe and give you some company."

Fleur retreated another step, knowing she'd taken too much of the woman's time already. "Don't think twice about it. Thanks again for a really nice evening—*Oof!*" she exclaimed as she backed into a warm, muscular wall.

Drake's hands were on her arms, steadying her from behind. At the same time, he called to his sister over Fleur's head.

"I've got her, Emma. I can drive her home."

Fleur's heart pounded too hard from the contact to gainsay him. And the last thing she wanted was to argue with her friend's brother in front of Emma, who was giving her a juicy contract for a catering job.

So she tamped down the surge of awareness and channeled it all into agitation, glaring at Drake as she stomped across a gravel road to where his pickup was parked near an equipment barn. She waited until he'd helped her up into his truck.

Once he'd closed the door behind her and climbed into the driver's seat, she whirled on him. "What do you think you're doing?"

Six

Excellent question.

Drake had asked himself the same thing only about twenty times since the offer to drive Fleur home had leaped from his mouth. What the hell had he been thinking when he'd skipped dinner to avoid her, spending the time berating himself for coveting the woman he'd warned his brother against? He was supposed to be finding a way to befriend her enough to convince her to sell Crooked Elm to him, a goal directly in opposition to avoiding the attraction he felt for her.

Grinding his teeth as he put the pickup in Reverse, he kept his focus on the rearview mirror instead of the woman beside him.

"I'm taking you home," he managed once he'd

unlocked his jaw enough to speak. "That's what I'm doing."

The sound of her windy sigh expressed the same exasperation he felt. He put the truck in gear and headed for the main road. Walking the back way between their ranches was only about three miles. The county route took longer, remaining on the outskirts of both properties.

"What I mean is, why would you volunteer for the job now, after how awkward the ride over here was?" Her voice filled the truck cabin, feminine and sweet somehow, even through her frustration. It made him think about the confidences shared earlier when he'd pressed her close. "And don't say it wasn't, since you went out of your way to disappoint Emma by not showing up for the meal she made. I know it was because you didn't want to see me."

He considered the question carefully while the headlights shone a path through the darkness. He'd always liked the lack of ambient light out here, the way the stars seemed closer. But right now, driving Fleur home, he focused on the woods close to the road, alert for critters that could jump out in front of the vehicle.

"I didn't skip dinner just to avoid you," he said quietly. "I needed the time to think about what you told me. It changes…things. Between my brother and me."

When she didn't answer right away, he stole a glance over at her. She stared out the passenger window, while one finger traced a slow pattern on the pane.

"I hadn't realized until tonight that your relationship with Colin was strained," she said at last. "I assumed that once Colin and I broke our engagement, things went back to normal between the two of you."

How much to say about the heated argument he'd had with Colin that day five years ago? Drake's first instinct was to keep Alexander family matters private. But given how integral a role Fleur had played—and that she'd be there when Colin returned for Emma's wedding—he thought it best to share something of what happened.

Besides, he had to start somewhere with building some trust between them.

"Everything came to a head for us the day I heard you two talking about the pre-nup. I told him about my concerns the day before I confronted you." He didn't like to recall the argument, but he dredged up some sound bites now in order to paint a picture for her. "My insistence that he was too young to marry and you hadn't been dating long enough turned into him rebelling against everything I'd tried to do since becoming head of the family. He accused me of planning his life for him. From the college he'd attended to the way he spent his weekends, since I'd expected him to continue pitching in on the ranch."

Drake had been angry, wondering how his younger brother could have the audacity to suggest *his* life had been plotted out for him. Did he honestly think Drake had been able to make his own choices? Everything he'd done had been to protect his brother and sister, to ensure their future. He'd forsaken a college scholarship and all but quit rodeo, giving up any serious pursuit of a sport he'd once been poised to dominate. Staying on the fringes, entering weekend competitions for prize money, had only rubbed salt in the wound of all he hadn't been able to accomplish.

"But Colin was twenty-three years old at the time, not a kid in school." She sounded puzzled, but she was facing him again, giving the conversation her full attention. "He was done with college. I thought he really enjoyed working here. We even talked about settling in Catamount for good."

Did she know how wistful she sounded? he wondered. The idea reminded him of his responsibility in breaking them up, and the new sense of guilt mingled with resentment that she should want Colin while Drake couldn't help thinking about *her.*

Turning onto the main road, his grip on the wheel tightened.

"Perhaps he only said that to be agreeable." He couldn't help the harshness in his tone. "He'd told me more than once he wanted out of the family business. I assumed it was because he disliked cattle ranching, so it came as a surprise when he bought his own spread two states away. Turns out it wasn't the work he objected to. Just me."

Despite everything he'd done to ensure his siblings were secure after their parents died. Colin had been fourteen at the time. He would have gone into foster care if Drake hadn't given up his own college scholarship to stay at home to oversee things. Not just his siblings, but the ranch, too. Thank God he'd been eighteen then. He shuddered to think what would have happened to all of them if he'd been even one year younger.

He hadn't expected thanks. He would have never made a different decision. But he would have never guessed that Colin would resent him.

In the silence afterward, Fleur's hand dropped lightly on his thigh.

"It might not have anything to do with you," she suggested softly. "My siblings ran to opposite coasts as soon as they could after my parents' divorce. I don't think they wanted to escape me so much as the site of their unhappiness."

He appreciated the idea. Would have found comfort in the words even, except that her hand on his thigh made it tough to think about anything but touching more of her.

His muscle tensed under her palm. Everything tensed, for that matter. His blood ran hotter around this woman, and there was no help for it.

So he was glad to spot the turnoff for her grandmother's house just ahead. The sooner he dropped her off safely, the faster he could stop thinking about exploring the sparks that flared brighter every time they were together. Another day, he'd figure out how to win her over enough to sell Crooked Elm to him. For tonight, he needed to retreat until he figured out how to deal with the unexpected revelation that a red-hot fire burned beneath their old animosity.

"All those months where you and I were on the road at rodeos all over the West—the bull rider and the rodeo queen—" he glanced over at her, a cool smile in place "—who would have thought we'd be the ones to keep the home fires burning?"

Her hand evaporated from his leg like it had never been there—as he'd known it would. Their enmity had begun on the road, from the early days when he'd teased her about how seriously she took her pageant roles, to later years when she'd pranked him by making a fake dating profile for him. She'd only been a kid—eighteen when he'd quit the rodeo circuit, and she hadn't been well supervised, with her mother or sisters showing up only sporadically.

He should have cut her more slack.

Now he missed her touch immediately. Yet he was also grateful for the reprieve, however brief, from this growing hunger to kiss her until they were both breathless.

"You didn't know I had a sentimental streak, did you?" she shot back, sticking close to the passenger side door as he slowed to a stop in front of her grandmother's house. "It was always tough for you to see underneath the spangled dresses and leather fringe, but it's there."

The last thing he needed was to start imagining the body under her clothes. Especially when those cutoff shorts had him fantasizing about her thighs all day long.

But her wry tone and tight smile made him feel like a first-class ass for not simply accepting the comfort she'd offered. But discovering he was more attracted to Fleur than ever was still screwing with his head, and he couldn't afford another breathless moment of staring at her lips, like he'd experienced earlier today. Better to send her on her way mad at him.

"If you say so." Braking to a stop, he glanced over at her before parking the truck. "Good night, Miss Silver Spurs."

He wasn't surprised when she slammed the door in his face.

Arriving at the Cowboy Kitchen just as they flipped over the sign to Open, her car full of freshly baked treats for the diner to sell, Fleur hoped she could maintain her running streak of avoiding Drake. Surely that would be a benefit of rising long before dawn to start baking—getting in and out of the Cowboy Kitchen without running into the owner. It had been ten days since Drake had driven her home after her dinner with Emma, and she guessed he was taking the same pains to stay away from her as she was from him.

She recognized his tactics that night when he'd dropped her off. Right at the moment when he'd showed her something deeper, something real, he'd shifted the heartfelt conversation into verbal combat.

Truly, she'd never seen him so clearly as she had at that moment. He hid behind the old quarrels as surely as she did—shoving aside any hint of tenderness behind the safety of contentious words.

The realization, and the empathy that came with it, had rattled her. His truck wasn't in the parking lot of the local eatery, however, and that had to be a good sign. She'd followed his suggestion and checked with the manager—who turned out to be Marta, her old friend from 4-H who also waitressed there—about stocking cookies, tarts and cakes in the display case a couple of times each week. Marta had been enthusiastic, and they'd test run some things last week.

Two days ago, Marta had informed Fleur everything sold out, and they were ready to order more. The order had come in the nick of time to pay some of Fleur's most pressing bills since she wouldn't receive the bulk of the payment for catering Emma's wedding until after the event. Even now, the first payment was contingent on a tasting that she'd set up with Emma for tonight. They'd finalize the menu afterward so Fleur could order everything she needed. The wedding was less than two weeks away.

And although both of her newfound income sources were connected to Drake Alexander, at least she wasn't working directly for him, the way she would have been if she'd taken a job at Cowboy Kitchen. This way, she was an independent contractor, doing business with one of his businesses, right? She didn't have to feel dependent on Drake, even though the rich rancher seemed to support the entire town of Catamount in one way or another. Even the local nature conservancy had sung his praises when they stopped by yesterday to make an appointment with her to discuss the diminished condition of wetlands on Crooked Elm property. She'd put them off for a couple of more days, certain whatever they wanted would be expensive when she couldn't afford to invest any more in the property.

But every day she spent working in her grandmother's kitchen made her wish she didn't have to sell Crooked Elm.

Now, stepping out of her rattletrap vehicle, Fleur turned to open the creaking back door to unload her carefully packed baked goods when her cell chimed. At six in the morning? Surprised, she tugged the phone from the pocket of her denim skirt to check the screen.

Jessamyn.

Her sister never contacted her just to chat. Knowing it was either business or an emergency, Fleur accepted the call.

"Hello?" She shifted to lean against the trunk of her car, careful to avoid a spot on the fender where silver paint and rust were both flaking away.

"Sorry to call so early, Fleur, but I wanted to touch base before Dad gets in the office." Her sister's voice sounded weary, which might not have been unusual for some women at that hour, but Jessamyn had long been a disciple of the school of hustle and grind. She thrived on long hours and doing anything to get ahead.

"It's fine. Everything okay there?" She tipped her head back to feel the sun's early rays on her face, the cooler air welcome after a couple of hot days.

She'd always loved the weather in Colorado. Even the hottest days were tempered by lower humidity than Dallas. She swore her recipes were better here, too, but that might have more to do with her mood than the weather. Not even Drake's presence in her life could diminish the joy she took in being at her Gran's house. She just wished she hadn't waited so long to return.

"Yes, but I wanted to alert you that Dad's been receiving mail from local conservation groups near Catamount concerned about land management practices at Crooked Elm. Were you aware of this?" Jessamyn's blunt way of speaking always felt vaguely accusatory, and Fleur had to remind herself not to take offense where none was meant.

Being raised in a household of warring factions definitely made Fleur even more prickly. It had occurred to her after her last exchange with Drake that her tendency to snipe and be defensive had shaped her relationship with him early on. But those rodeo years that he liked to tease her about had been hell for her. Did he think she enjoyed all the times she'd dressed up in gowns she found at consignment shops to compete for prizes to afford her education? Even before her dad had cut off support to her, he'd warned her he wouldn't be helping with college. She'd hit the pageant circuit hard at sixteen.

In theory, Fleur had loved a lot of things about rodeo life. Behind the scenes had a culture of its own, however, and in her experience, it hadn't always been warmhearted and supportive. She shook off the mental wandering and focused on Jessamyn's question.

"Gran's tenant for the rangelands mentioned it to me." She didn't say anything about the visit from the local conservation group yet, keying in on the other piece of information that troubled her. "Why is mail going to Dad about Crooked Elm?"

The last thing they needed was for their father to be involved in how the property was managed until they sold it. Antonia had been very deliberate about willing the place to her three granddaughters, not her son who had turned his back on the old ranch long ago.

"I don't know." Jessamyn sounded puzzled. "I've been meaning to look into that. Maybe he's paid tax bills for Gran before."

Worry tickled along her senses since her sister didn't sound confident of the answer.

"Dad won't contest the will or anything, right? Isn't it too late for that?" She did not know how the legalities worked, assuming her grandmother's will would be enough for them to move forward.

"Technically, no. It's not too late since the court still has to have a hearing to confirm the will, but I'm sure everything is in order." Jessamyn huffed out a windy sigh. "Anyway, I'm trying to clear my schedule for next month, so I can work on the house before we put it up for sale once the estate is settled. In the meantime, I'm sending a picture of this letter so you can look into it. We don't want any legalities to tie up the property."

She plucked at her blouse with nervous fingers, hoping Jessamyn was just being overly cautious. A big green tractor rumbled past on the main road, making it hard to hear anything else for a moment.

"I'll figure it out," she said once the farm vehicle had moved away, the words more to reassure herself than as an actual statement of fact. "Thanks for letting me know."

On the other end of the call, her sister seemed to hesitate before answering.

"If it's too much for us, Fleur, we can ask Dad for help. He hires companies all the time to fix up houses—"

"Never." She bit the word out with more vehemence than she'd intended considering Jessamyn had long supported their father's stance on most everything. "He would do it to help you, Jess, but he would resent every cent that might benefit Lark or me."

Her sister's tone softened. "I don't think that's true anymore."

Biting her lip against the urge to argue, Fleur straightened away from her car and turned back to the stacks of plastic containers buckled into the safety harness.

"Either way, I would never accept his help now." He'd abandoned her when she'd needed a father's love, never showing up for any of her pageants or putting in time to chaperone her when she'd been tying herself in knots to earn college scholarships. Was it any wonder she'd developed a reputation as a haughty ice queen on the rodeo circuit? She'd had her reasons for seeming untouchable, a kid's coping mechanism for unwanted attention. Then again, maybe if she'd kept up the old hauteur to avoid attention, she wouldn't have had to quit her last job, where the kitchen manager had no concept of personal space. Or keeping his hands to himself. "Unlike Dad, I don't believe the almighty dollar solves every problem."

He'd been more concerned with guarding his fortune against his ex-wife and anyone who sympathized with her. And while Fleur tried not to be the kind of cringeworthy adult who blamed her problems on her parents, Fleur had found herself frequently unpacking baggage from that time in her life, from her father's decision that she wasn't worthy of recognition as his daughter. At least now, she was more aware of her own behavior because of it.

Recognizing it didn't always make her change, however.

"Heard and understood," Jessamyn retorted, the biting tone sounding more like her old self. "Far be it for anyone in this family to do things the easy way."

After saying goodbye, Fleur tucked her phone in her pocket and withdrew the first stack of boxes filled with cookies and tarts to bring inside the restaurant. While she'd been standing in the parking lot, two other cars had pulled in with patrons for the diner, and the scent of ham and bacon wafted on the breeze every time the door opened.

Unwilling to miss out on potential sales because she'd been gabbing with her sister, Fleur hurried inside with the containers, thanking Marta as the other woman appeared in time to open the front door for her, her dark ponytail bouncing on one shoulder in time with her energetic walk.

"Good morning," Fleur greeted her, taking care not to jostle her cargo as she wound her way through the tables toward the counter, where an old-fashioned bakery case had been scrubbed clean. "I still have more outside."

A handful of patrons glanced her way while a George Jones tune played softly over hidden speakers. The scent of coffee hung in the air while pans and utensils banged in the back. Fleur missed working in a restaurant, the rhythms of a shared kitchen workspace calling to her.

One day, if she could sell Crooked Elm, she really had a shot at opening her own place.

"Do you need help? I can dart out for a minute—"

She shook her head once she'd settled the boxes near the case. "That's okay, but thank you. It's a huge help to have you get the door."

"I'll follow you out, then." Marta paused to pick up a coffeepot behind the counter so she could refill a patron's cup. "I'm right behind you."

Fleur nodded, respecting the other woman's ease with doing multiple things at once, a coveted skill in any busy eating establishment. "Sounds perfect."

"And be thinking about what you want for breakfast. Drake said to give you a meal on the house whenever you brought us items to sell." As she spoke, Marta had already moved to start filling the bakery case with fresh pastries.

Fleur noticed an older couple getting up from their seats to check out the wares, but her pleasure in their obvious interest was diminished by Marta's words.

Had Drake told Marta to buy from Fleur in the first place? She'd been okay with him recommending that she try Cowboy Kitchen as an outlet, but she was less comfortable with him paving the way for her if she hadn't earned it. And she definitely wasn't accepting meals from another man who thought he could buy his way through life.

Especially one who also assumed that Fleur could be bought. Just as he'd thought when he found out about her engagement to Colin. Drake had been so sure she only wanted to marry him for financial security.

Pushing her way out the front door, bells chiming, Fleur retrieved the rest of her wares. Yet her joy in the act was diminished with the possibility of Drake's interference weighing on her.

As much as she didn't want to see him again—attraction be damned—she really should clear the air with the man who seemed to have all of Catamount under his thumb. She would explain that she didn't need his help securing work, or feeding herself, for crying out loud. Besides, she still wanted to ask him more about the local conservation efforts since Josiah Cranston had implied Drake was something of an expert.

So, after unloading the last stack of baked goods and politely declining Marta's efforts to feed her, Fleur stepped out into the sunshine and got out her phone again.

Without giving herself time to overthink it, she found Drake's contact information. He'd insisted she take it almost a decade ago when he'd appointed him-self her disapproving guardian on those times they'd ended up at the same rodeos.

Even then, he'd been judgmental and condescend-ing toward her, convinced everything she did was to make a spectacle of herself. Why would she have thought he'd changed just because he made her heart race faster now?

Thumbs flying over the screen, she typed:

Emma's tasting for the reception is tonight at Crooked Elm. I hope you'll join us.

And sent it before she could have time to regret it.

Seven

Standing outside the goat pen at Crooked Elm Ranch, Drake scratched the head of a floppy-eared Nubian in the hope of quieting her. The mottled brown-and-white animal had been bleating with urgency during the last half hour of the tasting Fleur had arranged for Emma. Drake had used the distracting calls as an excuse to let his sister make her selections for the reception menu.

Or maybe he'd just latched on to the first excuse he could think of to step away from the draw of their hostess.

While two other goats ambled over to greet him—both black and white—Drake felt his attention yanked back to the picnic table draped in a sunny yellow tablecloth, where Fleur reviewed wedding cake ideas on a tablet. She wore a white tank top and a pale green skirt printed with flowers that ended just above her knees. Her copper-colored hair was tied into a low ponytail with a sheer pink scarf. He'd spent half the tasting thinking about untying the fabric and teasing the ends over her skin.

But the other half of the time, he'd spent forcing himself to admit that not only had he misjudged her in the past, he'd also failed to recognize that she'd become a force to be reckoned with in her own right.

He'd been so sure she'd only rolled into town to serve her own ends by selling off the ranch to the highest bidder so she could count up her profit. Yet she'd surprised him by moving into the place for the summer and connecting with the residents of Catamount again. After seeing the effort she'd put into baking, he'd insisted Marta give her an outlet for her goods at Cowboy Kitchen. And he wasn't the only one who'd noticed her talents. He'd heard from Emma that she'd booked small catering jobs with two of her friends—someone's baby shower and a retirement party for a local farmer.

Yet until this evening, when he'd watched Fleur in sales mode going over the possibilities for Emma's wedding foods, he hadn't really acknowledged that she possessed far more drive and determination than he'd ever given her credit for. She'd achieved a lot in five years, and her skill for cooking came through in her discussion of preparation and presentation. She wasn't catering just to make a buck. She was clearly passionate about it.

"They like you!" Fleur called over to him. She and Emma had both lifted their eyes from the tablet to watch him pet the three jostling goats. "This is the most content they've been since I got here."

The remark brought to mind how long she'd been in town. What kind of job had she left behind in Dallas that she didn't need to return yet?

"I'm not bad with animals," he observed lightly, wishing for a moment that he possessed some of the same ease with people.

His brother, namely. But now he also wished he had a way to prove to Fleur that his sole purpose in life wasn't just to give her a tough time. He didn't want to be continually at odds with her. He simply found it convenient at the times when the thought of tasting her proved so all-consuming he didn't know how else to handle it.

Before she could reply, Emma's fiancé, Glen, arrived, jogging across the backyard in his cargoes and a polo with his ranch's brand printed on the pocket, as if he'd only just finished up his work.

Leaving the goats to their own devices and giving time for Glen to be caught up on the wedding menu, Drake strolled the perimeter of the yard, where Fleur's handiwork was evident. The last time he'd visited Antonia at Crooked Elm, the birdbath fountain had been caked in moss and the perennials surrounding it were a wild thicket. But the stonework had been cleaned, and the water feature restored so that it babbled softly. New plants mingled with old ones that had been thinned out and separated, a fresh layer of mulch protecting the soil.

Beyond the birdbath, a firepit had been raked clean and the rocks reset. The heavy wooden furniture surrounding it had been recently painted.

All of it made the setting for Fleur's sales pitch that much more appealing. She'd set out tall candles surrounded by glass globes to protect them from the breeze, and as the daylight faded into early evening, the candlelight gave the yard a romantic vibe.

"Are you done working your Doctor Doolittle magic on the goats?" Fleur's voice sounded just behind him, alerting him that she must have stepped away from the engaged couple for the moment. Perhaps she noticed him swiveling his attention back to his sister, because Fleur explained quickly, "I thought I'd give them some privacy to talk over my menu ideas. I don't want your sister to feel obligated to accept my suggestions just because we're friends or—for any reason."

His gaze stuck on her silvery-gray eyes as she turned to him, and he wondered if she'd always been thoughtful, and he'd just been too stubborn to recognize it. He scraped a hand over his jaw, seized with the need to touch her again. He hadn't forgotten how she'd felt tucked up against him in the saddle that day. How soft her skin had been when his thumb had brushed a bare patch at her waist.

"I was surprised you invited me tonight." His voice had dipped an octave, his thoughts getting the better of him. "Especially after how we parted last time."

He'd sniped at her to put distance between them, recognizing he was in danger of kissing her otherwise.

"I have a couple of things I hoped to discuss with you." She peered over her shoulder to where Emma and Glen studied the tablet together, their heads close as they sat side by side at the picnic table. Then Fleur looked up at him again. "Privately. Would you be able to stay after Emma finishes up? I'm guessing Glen is already signing off on the food items she selected."

His blood heated at the thought of being alone with Fleur, even though he knew she wouldn't have anything remotely intimate in mind. Still, just being around her amped him up.

"That's a safe bet." Drake had noticed the two of them seemed like-minded in many ways. It was one of the reasons he'd given the guy his approval to ask for Emma's hand. He took his role as head of the family seriously, and that meant ensuring his sister's happiness. "And as long as Glen can drop Emma back at home, I'll stay."

Even though it was surely unwise. Even though he'd told himself it would only worsen his relationship with his brother to spend time with Colin's former fiancée.

Fleur's shoulders relaxed a fraction.

"Thank you." Nodding, she seemed relieved at his quick agreement. As if she'd been worried he wouldn't give her an audience. The idea made him feel like a heel. "I'll just go see if they're ready to wrap things up."

Drake watched her walk away from him, his eyes drifting to the sway of her hips despite his best intentions.

He was going to need all his restraint to keep his hands off her. And he refused to fall back on the old knee-jerk method of bickering like a couple of kids. She deserved better than that.

But considering how long the attraction had been simmering inside him, he feared the slightest wrong move could start an inferno they wouldn't be able to ignore.

Fifteen minutes later, the tasting appointment had concluded and Fleur had a signed contract in her possession for Emma Alexander's wedding reception. Thankfully, the income would allow her to pay the bills this month and give her more time to work out her next steps. After thanking the future bride and groom, she stood in her driveway beside Drake to wave goodbye to them.

Glen would accompany Emma home, so that Drake could remain behind to speak to her, just as she'd requested. That should be a good thing. Except, as Glen's black extended-cab pickup vanished in a cloud of dust and country rock music, Fleur became more aware of Drake's muscular frame just behind her. His shoulders cast a shadow on her back, preventing the last rays of the sun from reaching her skin as it slipped lower in the sky. A shiver tripped over her, and she couldn't even pretend it was because of a chill in the air.

Her senses attuned to his presence. His deep, even breathing. A hint of his pine and musk scent. A thrill shot through her at the way her pulse zipped faster, even when she knew she had to ignore the signs of her body's obvious attraction to the man.

She hadn't called him here tonight for that.

"Thank you for staying," she said crisply as she turned to face him.

And promptly confronted a whole new set of compelling Drake attributes. His dark eyes locked on hers, searching. Was it her imagination, or did they lack some of the judgment they normally contained anytime he looked at her?

A frivolous thought. Wishful thinking that only distracted her from her purpose.

"Would you like to take a seat?" she blurted, needing to break the connection. Desperate to have the conversation ended so she could send him on his way before she allowed herself to be hypnotized by that magnetic gaze of his.

"Sure. Thank you for agreeing to cater the reception," he returned, shoving his hands in the pockets of his dark jeans. He still wore a black Stetson tonight, but he'd traded his boots for loafers. A white T-shirt and a subtly patterned gray-and-black sport coat, custom-tailored to his athletic form, reminded her that there was more to him than a bull rider. "It makes me happy to see Emma so pleased with the wedding arrangements."

He walked with her toward the picnic table, the candles inside the hurricane lamp flickering golden as the sky began its evening shift from pink to violet. There was rain in the forecast tonight, but so far the cloudy sky only made the sunset prettier.

The sincerity in his tone shouldn't have surprised her. She knew that Drake took his brother's and sister's happiness seriously, since she'd once been a casualty of that protectiveness once herself.

Still, she couldn't help the warmth that stole through her at having won this demanding man's approval in at least one area. She hadn't sought it. But considering how often she'd fallen short of earning praise from anyone in her own family, having Drake notice her efforts felt…nice.

"It's my pleasure." She stopped near the picnic table and turned her back to it so she could use the bench while facing away from the work surface. "I'll do everything in my power to ensure my responsibilities for that day exceed her expectations."

Drake took a seat on the same side, but he straddled the bench to face her directly, laying one arm along the table.

"But I'm guessing you didn't ask me to stay behind so we could discuss the wedding plans," he observed drily, and she welcomed the challenge in his voice.

Why was it so much easier to talk to Drake as her adversary?

"And you would be correct." Crossing her legs, she shifted toward him. "There are two reasons I needed to see you. First, to ask if you directed Marta to purchase food items from me in the hope of securing my good will in potentially selling Crooked Elm to you."

He reared back at the words. "Excuse me?"

"You didn't do that?" She thought his surprise seemed genuine.

Was it possible he hadn't been using their financial disparity to his advantage? She knew it was a hot button for her after her father's games with money.

"Of course not." He took off his Stetson and set it on the far side of the picnic table before tunneling impatient fingers through his hair. "Marta and the cook, Stella McRory, have autonomy over there. I wouldn't know the first thing about running a diner."

"Because Marta told me you said she should feed me when I bring baked goods," she added, distracted by the flexing of his square jaw. The hint of bristle made her wonder what his face would feel like against her palm.

Not that she would ever find out.

"I also set the employees up with better health insurance and comped one meal a day for everyone who works there. I won't apologize for good employee retention tactics, or for making sure local suppliers like working with us."

"Marta seemed really pleased to have a 401(k)," she remarked, recalling the other woman's pride when she'd said as much.

"There you go." He nodded, seeming satisfied. Vindicated. Then his expression softened. "I had no ulterior motive when I told Marta to extend you a courtesy meal. Though I guess I can't be surprised you would assume the worst of me, given our history."

"It's not just our history that made me uncomfortable with the idea." She flexed her toes inside her metallic silver sandals, noticing that her pink nail polish had faded. She'd been so busy for the past week and a half, she went to bed exhausted every night, with little time for anything but work. "My father enjoys flexing the power of his financial might in front of people. Especially Lark and me."

"I'm not sure the cost of a couple of fried eggs and toast at the diner would be an impressive display of my net worth if I were that kind of guy." The teasing note in his voice made her smile despite herself. "It's just a gesture, plain and simple."

"Right. Sorry to misread that." She didn't mention the other incident in her life that made her wary of men with power over her financial future. Her creep of a former boss wasn't worth bringing up.

The silence stretched for a moment while the katydids clicked and called in the nearby bushes. The sound was peaceful, making her realize the goats must be content now, too. All was quiet in their pen.

"You said there were two things?" Drake prompted a moment later. He slid the hurricane lamp closer to them on the picnic table, casting his features in a sudden golden glow.

All at once, a vivid memory slammed into her

brain from the days when they'd attended some of the same rodeos. They'd been in Evergreen, Colorado, and Fleur had been excited about her chances in the princess pageant for the younger age group, plus both her mother and Lark had been able to attend with her. Having her oldest sister nearby had made the whole event less stressful, since Fleur could focus on her performance, her riding and her presentation instead of the inevitable logistics of food, lodging and transportation to the various events. She'd been particularly happy after doing well in the horsemanship competition, and Lark had taken her to sit in the stands near some people she knew from Catamount—including Drake.

Lark was Drake's age, seven years older than Fleur. That had seemed a lifetime apart when she'd been fifteen. But Drake had praised Fleur's riding that night, and for one evening at least, hadn't seemed judgmental. She'd even been a little starry-eyed that he'd paid attention to her at all.

Until one of Lark's friends breezed into the group, draping herself across Drake's lap like she owned real estate there. The raven-haired woman had kissed him full on the mouth before stage-whispering to Lark that she was ready to take Drake back to her hotel so she could get the *real* rodeo started. Drake had chastised the bold brunette, his eyes flicking to Fleur, making her aware it was *her* fault that he had to rein in his girlfriend.

A shiver pulsed up her spine now at the memory that had no business flashing across her thoughts now.

"Fleur?" Drake's straight, dark eyebrows scrunched in confusion. "Are you okay?"

"Yes." She nodded jerkily, wishing she could shove aside the vision of Drake giving some random woman the ride of her life. "Um. I've heard you're a bit of an expert on the local conservation efforts."

Her voice sounded funny. Too high and thin.

As if she'd been having inappropriate thoughts of the man she would prefer to hate.

"It would be a stretch to say I'm an expert, but I've certainly invested in measures to preserve the natural ecosystem wherever possible. Good land management benefits the cattle, the land, native species—the list goes on. Why do you ask?"

"Well, I have reason to believe that—"

His shin grazed her calf as he stretched his legs.

"Sorry," he said automatically, gaze snapping to hers.

The momentary touch was like connecting an electrical circuit, the heat of his body apparent right through the fabric of his pants.

Her breathing quickened, the rapid intake of breath sounding loud in her ears when the only other sound was the katydid concert.

"I'm worried Crooked Elm is in violation of some environmental initiatives." She grabbed on to the conversation like a lifeline, confident there was nothing remotely sexy in the topic. "Jessamyn told me my father has been receiving mail from an agency that threatened citations on a few counts, but from what I could gather, they're most concerned about the creek."

She'd reviewed the letter Jessamyn had forwarded, but there were references to other regulatory documents she hadn't unearthed yet.

Drake nodded. "Antonia's tenant lets his cattle range too close to the water. The damage he's doing is going to take years to fix."

"You think that's it?" The problem seemed simple to fix if she spoke to Josiah Cranston. Then again, the surly rancher might not be amenable to changing his practices now.

What she needed to do was give him notice of the lease termination.

A cold breeze kicked up from the east, blowing her hair along her shoulders. She tucked a strand behind one ear to keep it out of her line of vision.

"There could be other problems, but I'm guessing that's the biggest area of concern. You should follow the creek next time you visit Emma and see how different the vegetation along it looks on your land compared to mine."

Frowning, she realized she would have bristled at words like that a few days ago. But she'd reached a new accord with Drake.

Even, she realized, a new trust. Because no matter their differences in the past, she believed in his passionate commitment to the land. He wouldn't steer her wrong about that.

When another breeze stirred even stronger this time, the ends of her hair floated dangerously close to the open top of the hurricane lamp. Drake darted forward, capturing the strands with one hand and pushing away the lamp with the other.

"Storm's coming," he announced, his voice gravelly as he kept her hair in his fist for a moment longer than necessary.

Then two.

Heat thrummed through her, pulsing in time with her heartbeat. She couldn't feel his touch, yet the thought of him tugging her head back with that hold on her hair turned her knees to liquid. Did something flicker in his dark gaze, or was that just the reflected candlelight?

A low rumble of thunder in the distance was probably a warning they should both be heeding. Instead, it felt like a drumroll overture for whatever madness was about to take place between them next.

She licked her dry lips as he resettled her hair behind her back. And then his hand was there, on her shoulder.

A warm, anchoring weight.

"Drake." His name left her lips in wonder. A plea.

And when another roll of thunder sounded, she felt the static in the air, the charged pull of the night and the man.

Except the thunder sounded different. Nearer. Like charging hooves galloping closer.

At the same moment the thought formed, Drake sprang from the bench. Breaking into a run, he called over his shoulder, "The goats are loose."

Eight

"Nimue, don't you want your dinner?" Fleur coaxed the small black-and-white goat, the only one they hadn't been able to capture.

Drake watched Fleur swing a bright blue pail to tempt the escapee, while the other two does inside the pen bleated and called, the yard partially lit by a couple of outdoor fixtures mounted to the barn. The brown-and-white Nubian—Morgan le Fay, he'd been informed—had returned to the enclosure as soon as Drake had herded her toward it. The larger of the black-and-white animals—Guinevere—had romped around the yard with more enthusiasm until she'd gotten distracted by a tasty patch of grass, and Fleur had been able to slip a lead around its neck.

Now only one holdout remained. He worked on

securing the pen where a board along the top of the woven mesh fencing had given way, while Fleur pleaded with the last jail breaker. Considering how his evening had progressed with Fleur before the animals escaped, Drake was ready to tie up the goat adventure. He could have sworn they'd been moments away from locking lips when a blur of horns and fur had streaked past them.

"I'm surprised it never came to my attention that Antonia named her goats after Arthurian legends," he observed as he hammered in a nail to fasten a replacement board into place. He'd been fortunate to find a stack of precut lumber inside the big barn and had made quick work of the job.

Another flash of lightning split the sky, illuminating Fleur's face as she cooed at the unrepentant animal. Drake set aside the hammer and turned his attention to helping her since a storm was imminent. He knew he should leave considering how badly he wanted to stay and find out if that kiss would still happen. Yet how could he have left her to deal with the broken fence alone when she already thought poorly of him? With good reason.

He'd misjudged this woman more than once, and now he wanted to offer an olive branch of his own. He would help her tonight, and offer whatever advice she needed to help her settle the land management citations.

Now Nimue looked ready to play, her floppy ears swinging as she trotted around the birdbath in the center of the lawn. He retrieved the lead rope Fleur had used with Guinevere and moved closer to the goat as the thunder sounded more and more ominous.

The air smelled like rain.

"Gran didn't have them for long. She rescued them two years ago from a shelter near Grand Junction." Fleur took a handful of grain and extended it, her hair whipping around her head as the wind picked up force. "She texted me a photo of them later that week, telling me she liked the idea of names that were regal and magical for the spindly little trio, convinced it would give them something to aspire to."

When the lightning lit up the sky again, Drake could see her smiling to herself at the memory. He only had a moment to enjoy the vision she made, wind wreaking havoc with her skirt, her natural beauty drawing his eye more than the days of spangles and big hair.

He was almost close enough to drop the lead rope over Nimue's head when the downpour started.

Fleur squealed at the same time the goat bleated, a chorus of feminine surprise. He was drenched instantly, the rainfall hard and cold. Time was running out, and he didn't want to chase the beast in the rain. Drake dropped the rope over the little runaway's head.

Thank God.

He raised his voice to be heard over the racket of the deluge sluicing over them. "I've got her. Go inside, and I'll make sure she's secure."

Fleur must have understood, because she bolted toward the abandoned picnic table, wet skirt clinging to her legs as she ran. Before he could lose himself in staring at her, he turned the opposite way, leading a humbled doe back to the pen, where she would have access to a warm barn and dry hay. Inside the enclosure, Drake tugged off the rope so the animal could take refuge with her friends. He closed and locked the gate before doing a visual sweep of the yard.

No sign of Fleur.

He hesitated for a fraction of a second, not sure if he should head straight for his truck or go inside to say good-night, but Fleur solved that dilemma by calling to him from a back door.

"Come in!" she called.

He only had an instant to note the white tank top hugging her body before he wrenched his gaze up to her eyes.

An instant that sent his pulse pounding.

Jogging toward the door, he paused under the narrow overhang outside the threshold.

"Are you sure—?" The unfinished question lingered for a split second, a world of meanings filling in the blank as they stared at one another, clothes dripping.

Any hesitation seemed overridden by her sense of hospitality because she gripped his wrist and drew him indoors.

"I insist." She let go of him once he was safely inside. After closing the door behind him, she passed him a white towel from a fluffy stack on a nearby deacon's bench with a tall mirror behind it. "At least dry off and wait for the worst of it to pass over. I appreciate you helping me with the goats."

She sounded breathless from running around in the rain. She'd discarded her shoes and now stood in bare feet on the gray ceramic tile floor. Water pooled at her feet, but she grabbed a towel off the tall pile and dropped it onto the floor. Her slender curves were outlined thanks to the soaked skirt and tank top; the picture she made burning itself onto the backs of his eyelids forever. She grabbed yet another towel, wrapping it around herself, but it wasn't fast enough for his liking. He forced his gaze away.

They stood in a dimly lit mudroom that he hadn't been in for many years. His younger brother and sister had spent more time than him playing with the neighbor's granddaughters in the summers that Lark, Jessamyn and Fleur had been in residence. As the oldest of his siblings, he'd been expected to learn the ranch business at an early age. Since his father was a self-made man, he'd wanted Drake to understand what it was like to work all the jobs on the ranch, from stable hand to foreman and—eventually— ranch manager—before taking over one day. Drake had chafed at pouring every available moment into the ranch during his senior year of high school, resenting that he never had a free weekend to do anything besides work. Now he would give anything for the chance to spend another day with his father.

But Drake shook off the unhappy thoughts as he mopped off the worst of the water on his face and arms. Beyond the darkened mudroom, Drake saw the bright yellow kitchen with mosaic tile countertops and an old fireplace built into the far wall.

"Is the fireplace safe to use?" he asked, seeing the log holder full of split wood. "I could start us a fire while you…dry off."

He needed her to change clothes. If not for her sake, for his.

She bit her lip, her face washed clean of any makeup, if she'd even been wearing any in the first place. Her eyelashes were spiky with water. The natural pink tint of her mouth turned a deeper shade of rose where her teeth stabbed the plump lower lip.

His focus lasered in on that spot, and he could almost imagine what she tasted like there.

"It's no trouble," he urged her, voice raking over his throat that seemed the only dry place on his body right now. "And we never finished talking about the land management issues you asked about. I've got a change of clothes in the truck, too. I'll just—"

His words dried up when Fleur bent forward to wring out the worst of the water from her skirt. Between the quick flash of thigh she bared and the soft bounce of her breasts while she worked, he wasn't sure how he'd make it through the evening. Not waiting for her to reply either way, he grabbed one of the overcoats he'd spotted on the rack full of pegs by the back door, and threw it over himself.

"Be right back," he barked over his shoulder, lurching toward the door.

But he already knew the cold rain wouldn't put a dent in the heat building inside him, all of it for Fleur.

* * *

An hour later, seated beside Drake on the long, traditional sofa upholstered in the same dark blue wool-blend fabric of her childhood, Fleur congratulated herself on successfully navigating the land mines of the evening with him.

He sat forward on the couch, explaining the cheapest ways to remedy the local waterway, his finger tracing an old map of the property. Once they'd both changed—her into a simple cotton knit dress that fell to her knees and him into dry, faded blue jeans and a black T-shirt that he'd had stashed in his truck—they'd moved to the living area to enjoy the fire more comfortably. The hearth was open on both sides so the kitchen and living room both received the heat.

Fleur had made hot cocoa and brought out almond croissants to nosh on, determined to keep her hands busy and her brain off the tempting man in her house. She'd spent the last hour peppering him with questions about potential issues with the rangelands that could impede the sale of Crooked Elm. Drake had been knowledgeable and helpful, explaining the problems with degraded water quality due to heavy grazing and concentration of livestock.

The map of the property had come in handy as he showed her the borders of where Josiah Cranston was supposed to graze his cattle versus the land he actually used.

Shoving aside her empty stoneware plate dotted

with a few leftover almond slivers, Fleur edged closer to Drake to see where he pointed.

"You mean to tell me that Cranston is using more of the land than he's renting?" Indignation swelled inside her as she recalled the man's face as he'd scowled and spit that day he came to the ranch house. "Effectively violating the lease?"

The fire snapped and popped in the hearth, spitting a red spark against the screen.

Drake nodded. "He convinced Antonia to lease it for a reduced price with the understanding that he'd install an irrigation system to fill that dry pond basin up here." He tapped his finger against the spot, and Fleur's cheek grazed his shoulder as she tracked the place.

Lightning crackled through her, making the storm outside feel like an afterthought. The scent of him— pine and leather, a hint of musk—made her want to bury her face in his shirt and inhale deeply. The low rumble of his voice in the quiet room vibrated along her senses, making her shiver. She repressed the need to scramble away from him, trying to downplay the jolt she felt from the contact. Instead, she tilted her head, keeping focused on the dried pond.

The broken lease agreement.

Right.

"He told me there was no irrigation on the land." She latched on to the memory of that conversation, knowing it was important. Critical to readying the Crooked Elm for sale. She should be thinking about that instead of all the ways she found Drake appealing now. "Do you think that means he never installed the system he promised?"

Indignation on her grandmother's behalf speared through her, along with a wave of guilt that she hadn't been around more to help. To see if Gran needed her. Instead, her grandmother had been trying to manage on her own with a swindler whose word she trusted.

Fleur cursed her pride for not returning sooner. She'd allowed her hurt and anger about the past to keep her far from Catamount, where she was needed.

"He definitely didn't install a system. And I've seen his cattle at the creek illegally. There is access to another reservoir up here." Drake wrapped a knuckle on another spot, far from the main ranch house. "But I've seen that system recently, and I know it's dangerously low."

"Did Gran know about all of this?" And if so, why hadn't she confided in Fleur? If she'd known, she would have returned to Catamount no matter how things stood with the Alexander men.

"I know she did. I spoke to her about it last fall to make sure she knew Cranston wasn't keeping his end of the bargain." Sliding the map onto the heavy oak coffee table, Drake picked up his gray stoneware mug and drained the remains of his hot cocoa.

"What did she say?"

He shook his head. "She said she wasn't worried about it. That she knew Cranston would 'come around.'" With a shrug, he met her eyes in the fire-

light. "She made it clear she didn't want me to confront him about it."

"I wish you'd contacted me." She held his dark
gaze, wanting him to know she spoke truthfully.
Notching her chin higher, she continued, "No matter our differences, I would have thought you'd know
I'd be here if she needed help." She hesitated, knowing he'd viewed her as shallow. Superficial. "Or if
you couldn't abide the thought of talking to me, you
could have messaged one of my sisters."

A log shifted in the fireplace, dimming the light
in the room from bright golden to a dull orange.

"You're right." His response surprised her. "I
should have gotten in touch with one of you." His
lips flattened into a thoughtful line before he spoke
again, with slow deliberation. "With you."

She hid the shiver that coursed through her at his
words. Forcing a smile, she had to ask, "You really
think I would have been the one you would have
messaged?"

"Maybe not. But it should have been. You spent
the most time here. It was obvious—even to me—
you cared deeply about your grandmother."

The recognition of that simple truth by someone
who would never give her credit she didn't deserve
soothed a little of her unease about what she'd just
learned. As much as it hurt that her grandmother
hadn't reached out to her, it also felt vindicating to
have Drake recognize her commitment to the one
person in her life whose love had been unconditional.

"Yes, I did." She tucked a strand of her still damp

hair behind her ear. The locks had curled, making it harder to smooth back. "But even so, I failed her. I should have done more for her, been here more."

"Don't say that." A reassuring hand fell on her knee, giving her a gentle squeeze. "Take it from someone who has chased himself through all seven levels of hell since losing loved ones. You can't spend your life regretting things you did or didn't do while they were here."

The grit in his tone told her that wisdom had been hard won. Painful. And, knowing the loss of his parents had to have been extremely traumatic, she slipped her hand over his where it rested on her knee.

"I'm sorry you've done that." She would have never guessed he'd have regrets about anything. He'd been all of eighteen when they died, and he'd always seemed like a model son, working the family ranch from childhood. "I'm sure your parents would be incredibly proud of you to see all you've accomplished here. Making the ranch a model of good environmental initiatives. Swooping in to save the local diner. Trying to keep your neighbors safe from unscrupulous tenants."

It meant a lot to her that he'd kept an eye on Gran, even if he hadn't contacted Fleur when he'd worried about Antonia. That he'd looked in on her touched Fleur. And suggested there was more to this man than she'd ever allowed herself to believe.

"I'd like to think they'd be proud of the choices I've made since…since then." His attention dipped to their joined hands, and she wondered if he took comfort from her touch, or if the contact stirred the same things in him that it did for her. "But at the time, I wasn't always the best son."

She guessed the quiet admission was one he hadn't made often. Maybe ever.

The room seemed unnaturally still, the only sound their breathing now that the fire had settled into a dull glow. Outside, the rain had eased into a steady, softer rhythm.

Something about the regret in his words plucked at so many of her own sore places. She understood how it felt to disappoint people you cared about. She was surprised that he did, too.

"Drake—"

He wrenched his head back up to meet her eyes again. "It's okay, Fleur. I've made peace with the past. Mostly. I just mean to say that there's no need to blame yourself."

She understood what he hadn't said. That he didn't want her comfort. He only wanted to give some. Which seemed in keeping with what she knew about this strong man, who'd not only ruled over a financial empire since he was eighteen but grown it.

Still, she hadn't expected this kindness from him after their acrimonious past. And she sure hadn't expected to be, for all intents and purposes, holding his hand right now while they sat side by side on her grandmother's couch.

Telling herself she needed to pull back now, before his dark eyes mesmerized her any more, she flexed her fingers to free them from his.

Just as his thumb circled a spot on the inside of her knee.

Slowly. Deliberately.

And if that didn't have her melting inside, then the twin flames in his eyes would have done the job. The electric connection that had been leaping between them all day—or, who was she kidding, ever since she'd returned to Catamount—returned with a vengeance.

She'd run fast and hard from it before tonight, telling herself that she didn't like Drake Alexander. That she didn't want to get involved with her ex-fiancé's brother. The one responsible for splitting up a relationship at a critical time in her life.

But right now, in the quiet living room with her guard down, her fears exposed and Drake looking at her like she was the answer to all his questions, she couldn't run anymore.

She didn't want to. This man had bulldozed right through her defenses, destroying the aloofness that had been her salvation in the past.

Part of her wanted to tell him as much. To rail at him for the confusion he made her feel. To blame him for showing her this side of him she hadn't known existed. But when she opened her mouth to say so, she found herself asking, "What are we doing?"

The words curled like paper in a fire, thin and disintegrating under the heat of need that had been building for weeks.

Drake shifted beside her, facing her fully, his hand never leaving her knee just below the hem of her dress. Still, his thumb grazed her sensitive skin, sending ribbons of longing up her thigh.

Higher.

"For years, I thought I would regret it if I ever let myself get close to you." The words were unexpectedly harsh. But then, he'd never sugarcoated anything with her, had he? She felt a momentary flash of hurt, until she locked into the first part of what he'd said.

"For years?" Had he known this was underneath the animosity?

Closing the gap between them, he shook his head impatiently. As if he didn't want to answer the question? Or as if the answer were obvious?

Her heart sped at his nearness. At what she craved.

"But now," he continued, his voice dropping deeper. His forehead touching hers. "I know I'll regret it more if I don't."

Nine

Just one taste.

Drake told himself that was all he needed. Okay, he ached for more than that. But a single taste was all he'd allow himself of this woman who tempted him more than any other.

One kiss, and he'd have the answer to questions that had haunted the corners of his mind for longer than he cared to think about. What if he hadn't brought Colin with him to that final rodeo? What if Colin hadn't driven Fleur back to Catamount after she'd failed to capture the Miss Colorado Rodeo title that would have given her the rest of the scholarship money she'd needed for college?

Drake had seen Fleur with different eyes that summer. She'd been twenty years old. No longer a kid he needed to protect. Some of her defensive armor had worn off by then, perhaps because she'd been developing a new confidence in herself and her ability to attend culinary school without her family's help. He'd recognized then that he wanted her, but he hadn't acted on it, knowing she had big dreams that didn't include Catamount or him.

His brother had acted, though. And the next time he'd seen Fleur had been weeks later when he'd discovered them engaged. His reaction had been out of bounds. Not just because he knew it was a bad idea for both of them.

But because he'd wanted her, too.

He'd ignored that hunger for so long, reminding himself of every fault he'd ever scavenged to find with her, that his appetite had only grown more urgent. Unavoidable. Undeniable.

Just one taste.

Fleur's eyelashes fluttered, her breath huffing damp and warm along his mouth as she considered his words. Her cheeks were flush with desire, with promise.

"I think I'd regret it, too," she said finally, dragging her gray eyes up to his. "If we didn't find out—"

Her tongue darted out to swipe along the upper lip. The glistening moisture proved to be his kryptonite.

His restraint shredded until he held on by a thread. Hunger to taste her had him salivating. His grip tightened on her knee by a fraction, squeezing gently. The red knit dress she wore skimmed her luscious curves the way he wanted to.

"Find out what, Fleur?" he prompted, body throbbing with need. "Tell me."

The corner of her lips curled up on one side. "What it would be like if we kissed instead of argued."

Yes. Relief that she wanted him twined with a new imperative to kiss her in a way she'd never forget. Fleur's hands moved to his shoulders, nails digging into the fabric of his T-shirt to grasp the muscle.

Testosterone gripped Drake below the belt.

Still, he stroked one hand up her neck, feeling the delicate warmth of her pulse beat beneath his fingertips. He would not rush this. He wanted to savor the moment, savor her. Then he cradled her jaw, angling her the way he wanted before his mouth descended on hers.

His groan chorused with her sigh as she sank into him, her back arching, so her breasts tilted up, pressing into his chest.

Just one taste.

He ignored the cautionary reminder in his head, fading by the moment, and hauled her slender form into his lap. Her hip grazed the erection imprinted on his zipper and the sound she made—half sob, half whimper—vibrated up her throat to rattle through the kiss.

Her fingers tunneled through his hair, pulling him closer, tugging on the strands. He calculated how fast he could have her dress off, as if he had any intention of taking this further. But he couldn't. Wouldn't.

But that didn't stop the thoughts blasting through his head as his hand slid up her thigh, careful to keep the fabric of her dress between his palm and her leg. Because the connection was setting off fireworks, and he knew he needed to get the moment back under control somehow.

Hadn't he promised himself he wouldn't take this any further than a kiss?

He cupped her hip, imagining her straddling him instead of sitting crossways on his thighs. A dangerous, delectable image. One that would be so easy to re-create in reality now.

Fleur swayed against him, soft breasts molding to his chest, the tight points calling to his mouth. He could do that much, couldn't he, without crossing the line? A taste there, too.

Palming one high, curved mound, he slipped his thumb inside the splice neck of the dress and dragged away the fabric to expose the red lace and silk of the bra, the rose-colored peak straining the sheer material. He fastened his lips around her there, drawing her in his mouth, sampling her flavor through fragile lace. He caught the vanilla and nutty scent of her perfume, a fragrance he always associated with her, and inhaled deeply while she rocked closer.

Closer.

"Drake." His name on her lips set him afire.

Her fingers scrabbled along his shoulders, looking for purchase or…pushing him away?

Releasing her, he edged back enough to look into her eyes. Assess what she wanted. Had he misread?

"Too much?" His whole body reverberated with need while he focused on her.

"No. Not enough." She spoke with quiet certainty even though her gray eyes remained passion-dazed. Lips still damp from his mouth.

Relieved he hadn't pushed an advantage, he savored the hungry look in her eyes that reflected everything he was feeling. Even so, the moment reminded him how close they were to taking this into a direction from which there was no coming back.

If they let this heat carry them away, would she resent him later?

"It wasn't enough for me, either," he admitted, trying to drag in a cooling breath. He scrubbed his hand over his face. "But I know this isn't why you asked me here tonight. I shouldn't—"

His gaze snagged on the swell of her breast above red lace. Whatever he'd been trying to say vaporized out of his head again, his pulse strumming an urgent rhythm in his blood.

Fleur's hand smoothed over his shoulder, and he forced himself to pull the fabric of her dress back into place to cover her up.

She closed her eyes for a moment. Swallowed hard. "Shouldn't? Or won't?"

"It's not about what I want." He thought of the devastation one wrong move could cause for her. For his brother, who would be in town for Emma's wedding soon. "I've already hurt Colin enough."

Fleur scrambled back, off his lap. "*Colin?* You think it was Colin who took the worst of it when you convinced me to call things off between us?"

Ah, damn. He regretted the words he hadn't thought through. Already he missed the warmth of her in his arms, and hated that he'd taken her right back to resenting him.

"No. I know I hurt you, too. It wasn't fair of me to make assumptions, to act out of—"

What? Anger? Jealousy?

He recalled the fire in his blood the day he'd come home to find Fleur and Colin in the dining room at the Alexander Ranch, his brother's arm around her while he kissed Fleur's forehead. A big diamond on Fleur's ring finger and plans for a new home in San Antonio spread before them.

"Go ahead, you can say it." Fleur shrugged a shoulder and tugged at the front of her dress, as if she could tuck herself deeper into the fabric. "You assumed I wanted to cash in on Colin's trust, and you treated me accordingly. Like a gold-digging opportunist."

Heat sprang up the back of his neck at an accusation that was all wrong because he'd willingly allowed her to think as much all these years.

"That's not true." He pressed the heels of his hands into his eye sockets and rubbed ruthless circles before letting go again. Met her flashing gray gaze. "I reacted badly that day because I envied him, Fleur. Even then, I wanted you, and I was furious with Colin—with myself—that I'd never taken a chance with you. And by then, it was far too late."

In the stunned silence of his declaration, Fleur's jaw dropped open before snapping shut again. She blinked fast, uncomprehending. Then, finally, her vision cleared as she seemed to understand all too well.

"You can't be serious," she half whispered. "You've never liked me—"

"I fought against liking you too much." He had been honorable. He'd set the right example for his siblings every damned day since his parents had died because his father had warned him in that last argument that he wasn't being a good role model.

"Why would you do that? Was I so horrible that you couldn't stand the idea of being attracted to me?"

"Hell no. You were too young for me." He'd been her defender. Her protector. He'd made sure someone was looking out for her when her family couldn't be bothered to watch over her, because even when they'd attended her shows, they'd been wrapped up in their own dramas. "By the time I could acknowledge that maybe you weren't too young anymore, you were with my brother."

Her nose wrinkled in confusion. "All the scowls. The put-downs. Why would you do that?"

"I was scowling at everyone who looked at you too long." Exasperated, he lifted his arms with a shoulder shrug. "And if I sniped at you, it was a misguided effort to keep reprobate cowboys from trying to get you alone."

For long moments, the crackling fire was the only

sound in the room while Fleur seemed to play this over in her mind.

"You told me to end things with Colin because of that?" The questioning look on her face said how she still didn't buy into what he'd shared. "Because of some unrequited feeling—"

"Absolutely not." He let her hear the unequivocal truth in the words, allowed them to sink in before he continued. "I didn't handle the situation as diplomatically as I should have because of my feelings for you. But either way, I would have still counseled Colin to think twice about marriage when you hadn't even gone to culinary school yet. You hadn't had a chance to live your dreams. It wouldn't have been fair of him then—of anyone—to tie you down."

Shocked at Drake's revelation, Fleur didn't know how much time had passed afterward when he rose from the seat beside her.

"The rain has let up. I should get going." He paced away from her and the couch where they'd kissed, his sock feet silent on the hardwood floor. "I'm sorry if I've overstepped tonight."

He was leaving?

Her whole body still hummed from the heat he'd aroused with his touch. His mouth.

And she didn't want to regret leaving things unsaid. She needed them to talk this through.

"You didn't overstep." She sprang to her feet, too, not sure what she wanted to say or what should happen next. But she knew that him leaving wasn't the best option. Not when she was in a muddle with her feelings and desire for him still weighed heavy in her limbs. "I'm just trying to make sense of what you said and…what it means."

She found it difficult to believe that this man who'd always pushed her away had—at times—wanted to pull her closer. And she couldn't deny that what he'd said about not wanting anyone to tie her down before she'd had a chance to pursue her dream had made her feel…seen.

Drake Alexander, her longtime nemesis, had understood things about her that no one else had taken the time to discover.

He paused near the fireplace mantel, his gaze going to a framed photo of her on graduation day from her culinary school. It wasn't a professional shot, just an image a friend had taken of her jumping for joy—tennis shoes visible under her graduation gown—near a downtown bridge close to the campus in San Antonio.

"It means that I've tried hard to do the right thing where you are concerned, but that I have a special knack for falling short." A self-deprecating smile curved his lips. "If you need help with the land improvements, you know where to find me."

He moved closer to the front door as if to leave, but she darted to stand in his path, her heart hammering against the wall of her chest.

"What if I need something else?" She didn't know what she was doing. Her brain hadn't mapped out a plan; she was just moving on instinct.

Because she recognized deep in her gut that she didn't want Drake to leave. Not with her lips trembling from the pressure of his mouth on hers. Her breasts aching from the exquisite pleasure of the kiss he'd given her there, too.

Desire flared hot in his dark eyes. It wasn't just the reflection of the flames from the hearth in his gaze. She could clearly read the same hunger she felt.

"That would be madness." His harsh words didn't deter her.

Especially when his nostrils flared, his breathing deepening the closer she came.

This man had been trying to send her running for as long as she'd known him. Yet tonight, he'd given her an insight into his behavior that she wouldn't soon forget. The heat behind all those old feelings was rooted in something more complex than simple enmity.

Something she wanted desperately to explore.

"You can't scare me off that easily anymore." She laid her palm on the warm wall of his chest. She felt the racket of his heart beneath her hand, the beating as strong and erratic as her own. "Especially not now, when I know what it's like to be the center of your attention."

Where she got her boldness right now, she had no idea. She only knew that if he left here tonight, she might never have the opportunity to delve into the attraction beneath his cool exterior again. And she craved that chance. Too many people in her life had overlooked her. Written her off.

Having Drake look at her this way now, like he wanted to devour her more than he wanted another breath, stirred a need in her that she couldn't ignore.

He dragged in a deep breath, and something in his expression told her he was going to push her away. Make some excuse about not touching her because of her brief, ill-fated engagement to his brother before he bolted for the door. But Colin had never looked at her like this. Colin never tied her in knots the way Drake did with just one heated look.

So she didn't wait for another argument. Even as a cool draft from the rainy evening filtered through the drafty door at her back, she wound her arms around his neck, pressing herself to the warmth of Drake's strong, hard body.

"Just one more kiss," she urged, speaking the words over his mouth before she let her lips graze his.

The growl of agreement he made rumbled through his chest and into hers, vibrating along her spine. A thrill shot through her, pleasure like a drug in her veins.

His arms banded around her waist, lifting her against him, sealing their bodies together. His mouth moved over hers hungrily, tasting, teasing, exploring every inch. She raised her palms to his shoulders, digging into the muscle there, holding herself steady for the sensual onslaught.

The kiss transported her, teasing a response from her that she hadn't known she was capable of feeling from a talented, generous mouth working over hers. But Drake kissed her like he had all night, like there was nothing more important in the world to him than finding out what made her sigh and wriggle, what made her go boneless in his arms.

His hold on her shifted as he backed her against the front door, his hands trailing down her thighs to lift them. Wrap them around his hips.

The position lined up her mound with the bulge in his jeans. Even with her dress and a layer of denim still between them it gave her a sweet spasm.

He captured her cry of pleasure in his mouth before he broke the kiss. She gulped in air, realizing she'd forgotten to breathe for who knew how long.

"You have no idea how long I've wanted to kiss you like this." His fingers tunneled beneath her skirt to stroke his way up her thighs. At the same time, his hips tilted forward, applying pressure right where she needed it most.

Fireworks danced behind her eyelids.

"Please, more," she murmured against his mouth, wondering if it was possible to wriggle out of the dress without ever leaving his arms.

She hadn't been touched this way since…ever. Because the encounters she'd had with other men were nothing—anemic simulations of sex—compared to this. And they hadn't even taken off their clothes yet.

"After I've dreamed about you for years, Fleur, I'm not taking you against a door the first time." The rough edge to his voice made her nipples tighten almost painfully.

And then, she realized what he'd said.

Would he really take her?

Would it really be the first of more than one time?

"My room is that way." She pointed toward the back of the house, to her old bedroom near the kitchen. "But I'd like to go on record as being fine with a first time against the door."

She flexed the muscles of her thighs, squeezing his hips and also rubbing their bodies together in a way that made her toes curl.

Instead of answering her, he cradled her chin in one hand, tilting her face up as if to study her.

"Are you certain?" His voice sounded ragged, raked over a dry throat.

As if the hungry ache was eating him from the inside out.

Or maybe she was projecting since that's exactly how she felt.

"Positive. I need you." Her words sounded every bit as desperate as she felt, but they must have satisfied him, because a moment later, he curved his forearm beneath her ass and carried her toward her bedroom.

His long strides rocked their bodies together, and her hold tightened on his neck. She tucked her forehead against his chest, rubbing her cheek over the warmth of his skin through his cotton T-shirt.

But he stopped at the threshold, not taking that last step.

"I don't have protection. Not even in the truck. I don't—"

"I have some," she admitted, splaying her hand

along the bristles of his jaw. "I've replenished a stash faithfully every year since—"

She'd gotten pregnant. Miscarried his brother's baby.

Was it her imagination or did a chill descend between them? It felt as if the molecules in the air around her all moved and shifted to accommodate this new information. But just when she thought he would set her on her feet and walk away from her again, he exhaled a long breath.

His grip on her thighs tightened.

"Good. We're going to need as many as you have."

Ten

Her wordless hum of pleasure was the sweetest sound he'd ever heard.

He would have battled his own need for her for Fleur's sake. He'd have forced it down if she didn't want him. Ruthlessly ignored it, no matter how much it cost him.

But he didn't have a prayer of refusing her.

I need you.

Her soft words still circled around his brain, a command he wouldn't walk away from. Not after the way he'd hurt her five years ago. Not after how long he'd spent denying his feelings for her.

So Drake crossed the threshold of her darkened bedroom, still carrying her in his arms. She remained wrapped around him, ankles locked around his back.

Every step he took across the cool plank floor created friction between their bodies, the warmth of her sex riding him.

"Where are the condoms?" He tightened his grip on her, needing to minimize the bump and grind motion until he was planted inside her. Deep inside her. He was beyond revved up from knowing that she wanted him, hearing the desire in her voice and seeing the way her eyelashes fluttered at each brush of his body against hers.

"I'll get them," she murmured, unwinding her legs from his waist so she could jump to the floor.

As she disappeared into a bathroom off to one side, Drake tugged off his T-shirt and strode deeper into her bedroom. It was a small space in a home that had been built in a different era, when a sleeping chamber was meant solely for that. But ivory walls and minimal furnishings—a full-size bed draped in a simple white duvet, a faded steamer trunk for a nightstand, a single chest of drawers—provided the necessary comforts. He tilted the dark plantation shutters that covered the lone window, allowing slivers of moonlight to fall on the bed.

He'd reached for the button on his jeans, flicking the first open, when Fleur returned. Her bare feet padded silently across the hardwood floor, her red knit dress swishing around her thighs even as it clung to her breasts where he'd eased open the bodice earlier.

Did she have any idea how sexy she was?

"I found them," she announced breathlessly.

He slipped his arms around her waist, hauling her

against his chest. Then he let his hands roam all over her, savoring the feel of her perfect-size breasts, the stiff points of her nipples.

"Do you remember the shared horseback ride?" he spoke the words into her ear, giving himself a view down the front of her dress where her chest rose and fell in quick, hard pants. "When I held you in front of me, just like this?"

Her hair caught on his whiskers as she nodded, her head lolling to one side in a way that left her neck exposed. Greedily, he bent to taste her there, kissing and licking his way up her throat. The warm vanilla scent of her intensified as he reached behind her ear.

"This is how I wanted to touch you that day." He dragged one shoulder of her dress down her arm, baring the red lace cup of her bra and the creamy swell of breast above it.

With one hand, he palmed the soft weight, squeezing and molding, teasing the tight peak with his thumb. With his other hand, he dragged up the hem of her dress until a red scrap of satin between her thighs was visible. He must have stared a second too long, mesmerized by the body he'd fantasized about so many times, because Fleur arched her back in a way that tilted her hips against his lap.

"You did?" She reached up to encircle his neck with her arms, the action lifting her breasts in a way that nearly brought them right out of the bra.

"Damned right, I did," he growled low, knowing he needed her naked soon. "And I've been imagining it ever since."

He cupped the V between her thighs, her damp panties clinging to her. He nearly lost it then and there, knowing she wanted him almost as much as he craved her.

"Show me," she urged him on, her eyes closed, dark lashes fanning over her cheeks. "You don't have to imagine anymore."

Something about the way she said it—her tone, maybe, or the languid movements of her hips as she rocked against him—told him how much she liked what he was doing to her. So he took his time making her feel good, drawing out the pleasure. Narrating it for her.

"I wanted to see these first." He hauled down the lacy cup of her bra, peeling it away from her breast. Then, trapping the nipple between his fingers, he squeezed lightly. "Find out what touches you liked best here."

He couldn't wait to lick her there, too, but he wasn't finished reminding her of that ride when he'd been pressed up against her, his hand brushing her bare waist from that too-short top that didn't cover her.

"What else did you think about?" she demanded, her legs shifting restlessly now. Her thighs twitched around his hand, where he clamped an uncompromising hold between her legs. "I find it hard to believe my breasts would have captured *all* your attention."

"You will not disparage these on my watch," he warned her, tugging the other shoulder of her dress off so he could fondle the warm weight. "They're perfect."

"Drake." She made the word a plea, swaying and undulating against him. "Hurry, please. More."

He'd never had a lap dance until today and now, he'd never want another after the way Fleur moved with a hypnotic roll of her hips.

"I want this, too. Have wanted it for so long," he admitted, slipping two fingers beneath the damp satin panties.

Discovering something infinitely softer. Sweeter. Hotter.

He captured the tight bundle of nerves at her apex and rolled it between his fingers, mimicking what he'd done to her nipple. She gasped. Tensed. Her whole body coiled and went still, waiting.

And then it released. Waves went through her body, and she relaxed.

He'd never seen anything more beautiful. Never felt more privileged. It humbled him. And only made him more urgent to be inside her.

"Fleur." He breathed her name on a hard exhale, his pulse gone wild. "Come with me."

She went boneless against him, and he scooped her off her feet easily, stripping her clothes off as he laid her in the center of that pristine white duvet. When she was naked, her copper-colored hair spilling over the pillow and her gray eyes following his every movement, he finished unfastening his pants.

Shed them and the rest of his clothes as quickly as possible. Every heartbeat seemed to echo with her name.

Fleur. Fleur. Fleur.

A rapid tattoo of urgency.

He ripped open the box of condoms and sheathed himself. On the bed, Fleur roused from her release, propping herself on her elbow to watch him. And having her hungry eyes on him only made him burn hotter to bury himself in her.

She reached for him as he climbed on top of her. Covering her. Her arms pulled him down, surrounding him in her softness and her scent.

He spread her thighs wider as he positioned himself, his gaze locked on hers when he nudged his way inside. Inch by inch he spread her, going slow and giving her time to adjust, but the fit was tight. Her breathing was fast, her arms clinging to him, and he would have sold his soul before he rushed her.

Still, his arms shook from the need to have more of her. Sweat beaded along his back. His forehead.

"It's okay. I'm okay," she chanted softly to herself as much as to him.

"Are you?" He tilted her chin to look in her eyes, wondering if he'd missed something. "Is it really okay?"

She nodded fast. "Yes. It's just—" She hesitated, sipping on her lower lip for a moment before she went on. "My second time ever. And it's been so long."

The revelation had contradictory effects. He wanted to redo the night and take even more time. Cherish her. But the caveman part of him that wanted to claim her—to imprint himself on her so that she'd never want anyone else—was a primal instinct that was impossible to ignore.

So of course, he *would* ignore it. Because he knew better than to act on the caveman side.

"Fleur." He held himself very, very still while he got command of himself. He should withdraw perhaps. Give her another orgasm.

But while he weighed the options, she arched her back and rolled her hips again. Her breathy sighs coming faster.

"There," she exclaimed, her gray eyes alight with new fire. New purpose. "I just needed a minute."

She thrust her hips forward in a move so unexpected he was pretty sure he saw the promised land for a moment.

"Fleur." Her name was a strangled sound in his throat, his body demanding more. Demanding that he move. Take her.

Never let her go.

"I'm good now," she vowed, her voice turning sultry as she worked her hips in another thrust intended to erase all his thinking faculties. "I'm ready."

And he hoped like hell she meant it, because nothing could have prevented him from surging deeper. Again. And again.

But with her slender legs wrapping around him, holding him there, he knew she needed the same thing he did. He cradled her hip with one hand, rocking her closer, finding the rhythm that sent them both catapulting over the edge. The squeeze of her feminine muscles began a moment before his control snapped.

The release rocketed from the base of his spine, steamrolling through him for so long he wasn't sure his legs could hold him up afterward. He sank to the bed beside her, unwilling to collapse on her but not sure he could bear his own weight for a minute.

In the aftermath, as the world righted itself again and his breathing slowed, he wondered what should happen next. He drew her closer, unable to resist the need to kiss her shoulder. Stroke her tangled hair off her face. She tasted sweet and salty at the same time, her clean skin now dotted with sweat. His and hers.

"You're thinking so hard, I hear the wheels turning," she mused from beside him, burrowing closer to lay her cheek on his arm. "Would you mind if we waited to talk about…what just happened? Table it until daybreak maybe?"

His stomach clenched at the words, even as he recognized she was giving him a grace period. A chance to get his head together before they had to face what they'd done tonight. Or—if nothing else—to at least enjoy this cease-fire between them and all the sensual rewards that could come with it.

Still, he couldn't help suspecting that she was already working out a way to pull away from him. And how messed up was it that he dreaded that thought, even as he, too, weighed how to extricate himself with the least possible damage? He might have screwed up the sale of the ranch. Probably damaged his relationship with his brother irreparably. And as for Fleur herself?

His stomach knotted tighter.

But he brushed aside all of that as he combed his

fingers through tousled auburn strands. Right now, he just wanted to lie by her side. Hold her.

"I never thought I would say these words to you, Fleur Barclay, but I agree with you one hundred percent."

Tomorrow would be soon enough to deal with the fallout that was inevitable from their night together.

Fleur wasn't certain how long she slept.

Her bedroom remained dark save for moonlight, and the rain outside had slowed to a gentle patter on the roof. The sound normally soothed her, but with Drake stretched beside her, his hand still cupping her hip even as he dozed, she felt a spike of nerves.

What had she done?

Shifting on her pillow so she could watch the man beside her, Fleur's gaze swept over his strong, square shoulder where he lay on his side. His body tapered toward his waist and hips, an impressive V. She wanted to reach out and trace that slope along his lateral muscles, but she didn't wish to wake him.

Not when she needed to think.

Because sleeping with Drake hadn't been any part of her plan. Ever.

She lifted her gaze to his face, where she could see the shadow of dark bristles along his jaw. The moonlight filtering through the shutters turned everything a shade of gray in the room, giving the moment an otherworldly feel. As if Drake were a night phantom who might disappear into thin air.

But that wouldn't happen. His presence was solid.

Real. He'd made her feel things she'd only dreamed of before given the way she'd put off sleeping with anyone else after the disaster of her relationship with Colin.

Who got pregnant after having sex exactly once?

Fleur, that's who. The only guy she'd ever been with intimately—before Drake—had left her pregnant. Then he'd walked away without so much as a goodbye, heeding his brother's advice to abandon her. No doubt the relationship with Colin had been a mistake. An unwise decision by her twenty-year-old self longing for someone permanent, a family. She'd been shaking when she told Colin about the baby. But after the first shock he'd been honorable, proposing marriage and letting her take the lead in announcing the pregnancy. He'd been scared, but would do the right thing. Even though he hadn't been in love with her—nor she with him. Not in any real way.

But knowing that now didn't fix the damage. Damage that Drake had played a large role in. Because after being disinherited and ignored by her father, Fleur hadn't possessed the best coping mechanisms for dealing with Drake's interference in her life and Colin's departure.

Hurt and grieving, she'd been a loner through culinary school, only to end up working for a kitchen manager who couldn't keep his hands to himself. Where was her strength? Her willingness to be a badass and fight for herself when the situation called for it? Filing a sexual harassment claim seemed like too tame a response to something that infuriated her.

Coming home to Catamount had awoken something inside her. Her grandmother's spirit, maybe. Or just a connection to the person she used to be before her family had fractured. Baking in the kitchen at Crooked Elm had reminded her it wasn't up to her to repair her family.

She could only repair herself.

Beside her, Drake stirred, jolting her from her thoughts. His fingers flexed on her hip where his hand lay, the warm pressure of his palm enough to remind her of what they'd shared earlier. A blazing hot connection. Possibly the kind that would burn her if she wasn't careful.

"Hmm, why are you awake?" he said in a raspy, groggy voice. "I thought we weren't supposed to be thinking deep thoughts until the morning." He dragged her closer, an effortless move with just one hand.

And what made that easy strength so arousing? Her heart skipped faster.

"Maybe I was just contemplating all the wicked ways I could wake you up." She walked her fingers up his chest, reveling in the way his muscles jumped under her touch.

"Why do I have the feeling you're trying to distract me with sex?" His hand skimmed higher, settling in the curve of her waist as his gaze searched hers.

"Is it working?" She dipped her finger into the notch at the base of his throat before tracing his collarbone.

"I'm definitely distracted," he admitted, wrapping his arm around her waist as one strong thigh slid between her legs. "But I won't let that keep me from talking to you if you're concerned about something." He stroked her hair from her face. "You looked worried when I opened my eyes."

She could feel his concern. It was clear in the way he looked at her. In the way he didn't seize on the sensual out she'd offered him from this conversation. Her heart turned over at the sensation of feeling…cared for.

Swallowing past the emotions that swelled inside her, she thought about how to express all the things the night had awakened in her.

"Do you remember that rodeo in town, right after my parents split, where I sang 'America the Beautiful'?" She felt sure he'd been there. He must have teased her about it before, but she couldn't recall for certain.

"All of Catamount remembers that day." His fingers traced idle circles on her lower back.

"I didn't know until afterward that everyone had the impression that I did it to call attention to myself. Some sort of ploy for the spotlight." She had been hurt by that. But then again, she'd never explained herself to anyone, either. Never fought for herself.

"It might have been the timing of the song more than anything." He ventured the opinion slowly, perhaps checking her reaction. "Your mother might have been injured."

Had she been?

It wouldn't have been serious or Fleur would have remembered, although a pang hit that the thought hadn't occurred to her at the time.

"I couldn't see well from where I was in the arena." The lights had been bright. The tension so thick it felt like it was crushing her when she'd heard her father and mother shouting at one another. There'd been no other sound in the whole arena except for their raised, furious voices. "I just knew they were fighting for the whole town to hear. It was so painful. So needless and wrong. I did the only thing I could think of to cover it up."

"You sang."

"I burst into song." Shrugging, she wasn't sure she could relate a nine-year-old girl's decisions in a way that would make sense to a grown man. "Not just so *I* didn't have to hear them, but so the rest of Catamount wouldn't be talking about my cheating father and my out-of-control mother all day. Or maybe I did it so my parents would be forced to listen to me for those two minutes where I was center stage."

Once the words tumbled from her lips—the last part a surprise even to her—Fleur wished she could call them back. Hadn't she wanted to find some personal strength? Admitting something that sounded so self-pitying hardly seemed like a good start. But before she could backpedal, Drake's voice rumbled between them, his chest vibrating against hers where they touched.

"You and your sisters navigated some rough waters when your folks split." He watched her with curious eyes, no doubt wondering why she'd brought up the story.

"We definitely spent too much time focused on their misery instead of looking forward." She should own that much without being self-pitying, after all. If she wanted to grow, to change, she needed to look back at all of her journey and not just the better parts. "But I always felt happiest when I was here. In Catamount."

"Because of your grandmother." He nodded, his expression clearing as if he understood now. "You must be missing her so much this summer."

"I am. But at the same time, I feel close to her here. I have good memories in this house, and I feel like being at Crooked Elm is helping me find myself after being a little lost these last five years." She'd run from her broken engagement, and from memories of the pregnancy she'd lost.

But staying away for so long had been a mistake she could never fix. And nothing would give her back that lost time with Gran, the person who'd loved her most.

"I'm glad to hear it." He trailed a knuckle down her arm, a lingering caress that sent a shiver through her. "It's been good seeing you again."

His gaze dipped to her lips, his hand lifting to cradle her face. He tilted her chin toward him.

But she couldn't kiss him without telling him her point. A decision that she'd only just come to tonight as she lay here tangled in the sheets with him.

"I'm not sure you'll still think that when I tell you I'm considering staying in Catamount." She steeled herself, ready to be strong again. To fight for what she wanted. "I don't want to sell Crooked Elm."

Eleven

"Staying. In Catamount." Drake repeated the words, giving himself more time to absorb the bombshell she'd just dropped on him.

Hadn't she wanted to delay a conversation about what had happened between them tonight? And yet she'd waded into a conversation about something with far more potential to splinter the fragile bond they'd forged together.

His pulse jumped in a more merciless rhythm than any bull he'd ever ridden, his brain searching for a response. Because while he wanted to be supportive of her, he could also see the potential for disaster. Between them. Between him and his brother if Drake continued to see Fleur. And as for his quest to purchase the land for himself to restore the waterway, a task he felt honor bound to complete in his parents' memory?

That had just gone up in flames.

"Yes, that's what I said." Fleur had gone still in his arms. "My catering business is doing better than I expected. There could be a viable opportunity for me here. Not just in catering, but maybe one day expanding into a restaurant."

He couldn't help a shocked laugh as he levered up on one elbow. "The profit and loss statements from Cowboy Kitchen would make you think twice about that. I only bought it as a kindness to the community—a way to keep a local business open."

She propped herself up on a pillow, her bared shoulders tense.

"Perhaps that's why you're not making a profit," she said carefully, seeming to take his measure as she spoke. "You're not passionate about the restaurant business the way I am. I can see real potential for the right establishment."

Her prickly body language told him he'd offended her, so he shifted away from that topic. There were a hundred other problems with her plan he could tackle, after all.

Swiping a hand over his face, he shoved himself into a sitting position, sheet pooling around his waist. "What about the land management issues? How can you address the impending conservation citations when you won't have capital to invest?"

The problems with the waterway on Crooked Elm property already had a tremendous ripple effect on the water and land quality at Alexander Ranch, to say nothing of the properties downstream from his. He had a responsibility to his cattle to take care of it.

"I haven't worked out all the answers yet." She gripped the edge of the duvet tightly in her fist, drawing it closer to her body. "I'm just exploring the possibility."

The wounded note in her voice came through clearly, and he regretted his approach. He reached for her, wanting to recapture the closeness they'd shared earlier, the scent of her still filling his every breath.

"You're right. There's time to figure out how to make it work." From where he touched her arm, he felt the tension still thrumming through her, and knew he needed to dig deeper. Try harder. "I can help you. There are some measures you can take with the land that require more sweat equity than cash—"

"You know what?" Avoiding his gaze, she slid off the bed, plucking her simple cotton dress off the floor before dropping it over her head. "I probably shouldn't have said anything yet. My plans are still half-formed at best, and I'm not ready to think through things like that at this hour."

"Fleur, I didn't mean to discourage you—" he began, hurrying to get to his feet and drag on his boxers.

Already, he missed the warmth of her nakedness beside him.

"Are you sure about that?" she asked softly, busying her fingers with the dress's sash at her waist.

"That definitely was not my intention." He settled his palms on her shoulders, wishing he could draw her back to bed but understanding from her body language that their time together was done.

For tonight, he reminded himself fiercely, determined not to let this one time with her be his only taste of Fleur. They'd shared something deeper than a physical hunger for one another, and he fully intended to explore it.

When she remained quiet, he took her hands in his, trying to reclaim her attention. He needed her eyes on him.

"I'm sorry. I was only concerned for you and the obstacles you might encounter." He lifted both her hands to his mouth and kissed her knuckles. "If I had to do it all over again, I would simply say that Crooked Elm suits you."

Finally, her lips quirked. A hint of a smile.

Or maybe just a reprieve for the night.

"Thank you." Her eyes searched his for a moment before she took a step away. "But since I'm wide-awake now, I think I'll start the baking for the diner. I've sold out every time so far, so I'd like to make more than usual."

He didn't need to see the clock to know that dawn was still hours away. But he clamped his teeth around his tongue to keep from arguing with her. To prevent himself from running his hands over her curves and tucking her against him so he could kiss her thoroughly.

He wouldn't give her cause to regret anything that happened between them. He nodded as he reached for his shirt, then pulled it over his head.

"It sounds like the rain has stopped." He continued to dress, keeping his tone light. Easy. Maybe a retreat now was wisest. It would give him time to consider his next course of action with the sale of Crooked Elm. And with Fleur herself. "I'll get going. But how about dinner at my place tonight? We should talk."

About her plans. About the wedding and Colin's impending arrival in Catamount. About what had happened between them tonight.

She nodded, but she was already heading toward the door.

"I'll let you know." Turning the handle, she stepped into the corridor before he'd even finished the last button on his jeans.

Drake had an uneasy feeling. He felt her pulling away, and they'd shared too much tonight to just turn their backs on each other now.

Facing her in the hallway, he didn't know how to express himself in words. So he gave her the kiss he'd been longing to have since he'd awoken next to her in her bed.

"I'll call you." He headed toward the back door, where he'd left his shoes, telling himself there was still a chance they could figure this out without either one of them getting hurt.

Without hurting his brother any more than he already had.

He had no idea how to carry out his parents' legacy with the land if she remained at Crooked Elm, let alone what kind of relationship they might have as…neighbors? More? The idea tantalized and tormented him at the same time since, no matter what tonight meant for their future, they needed a plan before Colin returned.

"Are you sure you want to handle this on your own?" Jessamyn asked Fleur from the tablet screen propped on Gran's kitchen table. "We can hire a third party to legally serve Cranston the lease termination papers."

Fleur paused in rolling out biscuit dough so she could look at her perfectly coiffed sister. Fleur had been working for days on the prep for Emma Alexander's wedding, baking and freezing anything that could be made ahead of time, shopping and organizing foods that would be assembled later. She'd needed to fill her time ever since the awkward aftermath of her night with Drake.

Why had she been foolish enough to confide her plans to him? And how much more obvious could he have made it that he wasn't thrilled with the idea of her staying in Catamount? Memories of his deer-in-the-headlights eyes after her confession had taunted her hourly since then.

"If I can cater a wedding for two hundred on my own," Fleur replied, swiping a thumb across the tablet to remove a flour smudge that didn't belong on Jessamyn's face, "I think I can manage giving Josiah Cranston a few lease termination papers."

She might have ended her night with Drake on an uncomfortable note, but she had every faith in his advice about what was going wrong on the Crooked Elm Ranch acreage. If she wanted to address the land management issues, she needed to begin by canceling the lease agreement with her grandmother's uncooperative tenant. Her sister had provided her with appropriate forms for Fleur to initiate the process.

"How's the wedding planning going?" Jessamyn asked, surprising Fleur with a question that wasn't business-related. "You look exhausted."

"I am a little tired," she confessed, thinking about her lack of sleep in the hours before she awoke early to bake for the Cowboy Kitchen. "But aside from that," and the recurring sadness over misreading Drake, she silently added, "I feel good about things. The wedding. Crooked Elm. Being here is filling a place inside me I hadn't realized was empty."

Funny how she'd pinned all her hopes and dreams on opening a restaurant, yet she loved baking and cooking right here more than she had anywhere else. And it wasn't just nostalgia for Gran. Fleur felt productive here. Sure of herself. Like she needed to come home to recover all the pieces of who she'd been and glue them into one whole.

She'd even had some good news from the Texas Workforce Commission. They'd taken her claims of sexual harassment seriously. Her old boss would never be able to pull those tricks on anyone else.

Seated in front of her office window with the expansive view of Central Park, Jessamyn looked thoughtful, her expression softening. "I've been thinking about what you said—that we should spend some time at the ranch this summer so we could share the legacy Gran left us."

"You have?" Fleur set aside the rolling pin, giving her sister her full attention. She hadn't really expected Lark or Jessamyn—especially Jessamyn—to give the idea another thought.

Her heartbeat quickened even as she told herself not to get her hopes up. Her sister probably just wanted to explain why it couldn't possibly work out with her schedule.

"I've thought about it a lot, actually. There have been some things here—small issues I'm having with Patrick…" She cleared her throat at the mention of their father's protégé and the man Jessamyn and been dating for months. "Nothing major. But I've booked a flight for the week after Emma's wedding. I didn't want to descend on you until you finished your catering job."

Warmth and gratitude filled Fleur's chest, but she tried to modify her reaction to fit her all-business sibling. If she squealed in joy or got teary-eyed about a possible reunion, she could probably scare Jessamyn into canceling.

After their mother's over-the-top emotional displays, Jessamyn had gone the other direction. Nothing messy for her.

"I'm so happy you're going to be here," Fleur settled on saying, meaning it with every fiber of her being. How many times had she despaired of having any semblance of her family together again? "Thank you, Jess."

On the screen, Jessamyn was already bending over her desk phone, asking an assistant to send in her three o'clock before she nodded at Fleur. "I need to get going. But good luck with Josiah Cranston, and the wedding."

"Thank you." Fleur gave a little wave to her sister before disconnecting the video call.

She would have returned to her biscuits—part of the Southern-inspired portion of the menu since she had suggested Emma serve a mix of appetizers at her evening wedding—except her phone rang.

Knowing the biscuits wouldn't bake themselves, she thought about ignoring it, but Drake's name was on the caller ID screen.

Again.

She'd dodged him since their night together, unwilling to hear him make any more excuses for why he didn't want her to stay in Catamount. But with the wedding a week away, she knew she couldn't continue avoiding him.

And maybe a part of her still longed to hear his voice.

"Hello?" Switching her phone to hands-free mode, she settled it beside the tablet and then lifted the round biscuit cutter.

"Fleur." He heaved out a long exhale that sounded…relieved? "I was beginning to think you were blocking my calls."

Her cheeks warmed, and she attempted to deflect that subject. "Just busy with wedding preparations.

How are things going over there? Emma must be working on the barn by now."

"She's in full-scale General Emma mode, issuing orders faster than I can carry them out." His tone, confiding and fondly teasing, reminded her of their time together chasing the goats.

He'd been kind to her, refusing to leave her on her own to round up the escapees and mend the fence, even though she'd told him she could manage. So much had happened between them. So much more than just the sex, although her thoughts had probably strayed to that most often over the past few days. Well, that, and how it ended.

"I admire a woman who knows what she wants." Fleur pressed the cutter into the dough over and over again until she'd used every possible square inch. "Now that I've had a few more clients for catered events, I can appreciate your sister's decisiveness all the more."

"Your business is doing well?" he asked, seeming in no hurry to get to his point for calling.

Her nerves twisted at the thought as she used a metal spatula to lift the biscuits onto a baking sheet. Because she didn't know what she wanted where Drake was concerned. She only knew that she couldn't risk hurt from him when she was only just beginning to find her footing again.

"Business is better than I would have ever expected." She'd gotten two more jobs after agreeing to cater the wedding. "Thanks in part to your sister. She's been great about spreading the word."

"I'm glad to hear it. Marta says the things you bring into the diner are always gone by noon."

She couldn't help the swell of pride about that as she slid the last baking sheet into the oven.

"The foreman over on Ryder Wakefield's ranch has started sending someone into the Cowboy Kitchen first thing every morning to bring breakfast to all the hands." Cleaning up the kitchen counter, she checked the time, hoping to intercept Josiah Cranston before he returned home for the evening. "Is there anything else? I'm planning to take a ride around the range roads to see if I can find Gran's tenant so I can formally let him know that we're terminating the lease."

"There's most definitely something else." His voice pitched lower, and the effect on her was immediate.

Her breath caught. Her skin tightened. Memories of how he'd looked at her, undressed her, played through her mind in a tantalizing show.

"Oh. Um. What is it?" She cursed herself for sounding like an overexcited teenager. Especially when he'd seemed so taken aback by the thought of her staying in Catamount.

She set the dishrag aside and lifted the phone to her ear, focusing solely on the conversation.

"I'd really like to make you dinner. Are you free this evening?"

"I don't know, Drake." She closed her eyes, trying to shut out the way the sound of his voice made her feel. The way it made her remember so many moments from their night together—from corralling goats to tearing each other's clothes off. "Is it really wise for us to get involved when…"

Trailing off, she guessed he could fill in the blanks for all the reasons it wasn't a good idea for them to see each other. She didn't want to make things any more uncomfortable for him or Colin at the wedding.

"It's a little late for second-guessing that. After our last evening together, I would say involvement has already happened."

She bit her lip, knowing he was right.

"We never got to talk about it afterward," he reminded her, his tone softening. "Dinner would give us a chance to do that."

"To talk?" she clarified, uncertain if she could sign on for anything more than that.

Even though just hearing him made her insides heat and her body ache for him all the way to the roots of her hair.

"Don't you think we should at least come to terms with it? Maybe make a plan for the wedding, so it's not hopelessly awkward." As he spoke she heard a soft noise in the background.

An animal snort, she guessed. But then, he probably spent a lot of his time around his cattle.

"That makes sense," she agreed, wanting Emma's day to be flawless. Not just because Fleur was doing the catering, but also because she really liked Drake's sister. "I can do dinner tonight, but first I need to visit Josiah Cranston. I want to put those lease termination papers into his hands so the clock starts ticking on his thirty days to vacate the property."

She needed to keep her distance over dinner. Just a meal to work out logistics for how to be around each other at the wedding, and then she'd return home. No dwelling on what had happened between them last time.

No kisses that set her on fire or orgasms that catapulted her into the stratosphere. She couldn't deny the disappointment never to feel those things again, but she also felt a deep resolve at what had to be done.

"That works out perfectly," Drake agreed, sounding satisfied. Also, in the background, a bleating noise.

A calf, maybe, since there were no sheep on Alexander Ranch. She shook off the musing that didn't matter and tried to get her head on straight for the evening. Keep her distance. Settle what happened between them, make a plan for the wedding. Move on.

"Okay. I'll message you after I find Cranston and let you know when I can be there." Even as she told herself she wasn't going to swoon at Drake Alexander's feet again, she couldn't help but warm to his offer.

She had to be careful around this man or she could wind up with feelings she wasn't ready to have for him.

"I've got a better plan. Why don't I drive you around the rangelands and help you find Cranston? Then I can bring you home with me." Another bleating in the background, and the sound of Drake shifting around the phone.

She didn't see the need to spend extra time with him when it would be difficult enough to resist him over dinner.

"That's okay. I'm ready to leave now and—"

"Excellent. Because I'm right outside playing with Guinevere." The deep timbre of his voice teased over her senses. "I'm ready to go when you are."

Twelve

Watching Fleur exit the house and walk toward him in her simple white T-shirt and cutoff shorts, a pair of scuffed brown boots on her feet, Drake couldn't help but think how at home she looked here. Her copper-colored braid lay on one shoulder, a wilted yellow ribbon tied around the end, as she paused to scratch the brown-and-white ears of Morgan le Fay.

When Fleur had first told him she was thinking about staying in Catamount, he had assumed it would be a mistake. That an ambitious chef from Dallas wouldn't be happy in this remote Colorado small town. But how many of his assumptions about her were based on their rodeo days when she'd held herself apart from everyone else? He'd thought she was too proud, too full of herself. But he recognized now how insecure she might have felt after her parents' split. He understood better than most people how much influence a parent's judgment could have over a person.

How many of his own decisions had been reactionary measures to his parents' request that he set a better example for his siblings? That one argument had so much weight because it had been the last time he'd spoken to them.

Whatever the reason for his old notions about Fleur, the truth was that she thrived in Catamount now. She'd started a business here. Connected with locals like Marta and his sister. And, maybe most importantly, her good memories with her grandmother were here. Who was he to chase her out of town because he wanted to buy her land? The idea stirred unease.

Fleur stopped a few inches from him, her lips curving in a smile he hadn't expected but was so damned glad to see. How many times had he thought about her since their night together, reliving every moment of having her all to himself?

"You might have told me earlier in the phone conversation that you were standing outside my house the whole time," she chastised, her gray eyes meeting his for a moment before sliding lower.

Heat surged through him before she snapped her gaze back up to his, her cheeks flushing just a little.

That one moment made the days apart hurt a lot less. She hadn't forgotten their connection.

"I didn't want to spoil the surprise." His hands

ached to wrap around her waist and pull her to him, but he needed to proceed with caution. "Should we go track down your tenant?"

He tipped his head in the direction of his truck in her driveway, the insects singing in the trees as the sun sank lower on the horizon.

"That would be great." She shadowed him as he led the way to the vehicle, holding the door for her to step up the running board. "If you want to make a loop around the property, I'll give him the papers when we find him."

"Sure thing. I saw his truck on the far western edge when I drove over here." He closed her door behind her and then rounded the front to climb in the driver's seat.

After starting the engine and pulling out onto the dirt access road around the rangelands, Drake's thoughts returned to his concern about buying Crooked Elm out from under her. He really didn't want to displace her or upset her.

And, what's more, a part of him liked the idea of her staying in town. Would they see each other more if she remained right next door?

She nodded. "I'm just eager to deliver the news and start the process of him leaving so we can figure out what's next for Crooked Elm."

He remained in low gear, mindful of his vehicle on a road traversed more frequently by tractors. He wished he could throttle his thoughts the same way he kept a rein on the engine, but he found himself asking more about the Barclay sisters' inherited spread.

"Would you consider keeping your grandmother's house and selling off just the lands?" The idea seemed perfect for both of them. So perfect that he couldn't stop himself from pressing the point a bit more. "That way, you could maintain your connection to the part of the property that means the most to you, but you'd still have some income from selling the lands you don't use."

When she remained quiet for a moment, he glanced her way to see her lips pursed as she seemed to mull it over.

"I hadn't thought of something like that. The house seems such a part of the land, it never occurred to me to split them up." Her attention moved to the green grazing pasture off to their left, empty of cattle.

"So you like the idea?" Hope sparked. If she agreed to the plan, he could improve the lands without running her off. She could stay here and grow her business.

They would have the time to explore their attraction.

"I can't say for certain," she admitted, trailing a finger along the leather of the interior door. "And I would need both Lark and Jessamyn to agree, no matter what we do."

"Of course." He recalled as much, but for the first time, he saw a viable solution. A way for them both to be happy.

His conversations with his sisters had suggested they'd be open to a sale, so he couldn't imagine them objecting now.

"There's Josiah Cranston," she announced suddenly, shaking him from his musing. "You can pull over up there."

She pointed to a wide spot in the access road, close to a pasture gate.

Drake spotted the old-timer's vehicle in the distance, prepared for resistance from the unethical rancher who hadn't honored his agreement with Antonia Barclay.

"I'll drive you closer," he pressed, seeing an overgrown road alongside the field. His tires crunched through the undergrowth, the tall weeds brushing the undercarriage.

Beside him, Fleur reached in the back pocket of her cutoffs to withdraw a packet of folded papers.

The lease termination.

She already had her fingers in the door handle when he braked to a halt. "I'll just be a minute."

"I'm going with you." He shut off the engine and reached for the door.

"No, thank you." Her voice was sharp despite the polite words. "I'd like to handle my own business."

"And what if he's upset?" He shook his head, his gaze going to Cranston, where the guy seemed to be finishing up a phone call and tucking the device in his shirt pocket. "He already cheated Antonia with the irrigation—"

Fleur's hand landed on his arm. Firm. Certain.

"I'll handle him. It's my family's land, and it's my responsibility now." Her eyes locked on him. Determined.

Drake didn't like letting her confront the guy by herself, knowing that Josiah Cranston wasn't a particularly honorable person. But he could see this meant something to Fleur.

Reluctantly, he nodded. "I'll be right here if you need me."

Still, tension knotted in his shoulders as he watched her walk away to speak to him. Did she have any idea how tough it was for him to let her go alone? Not that he expected the surly rancher would lash out physically or anything. But Drake recognized that his protective streak had strengthened since his parents' deaths. It wasn't easy for him to watch people that he cared face anything he perceived as a potential danger.

That's why it had been impossible for him to let Colin marry Fleur without saying something. Even Emma had needed to tell him to back off sometimes. Now, with Fleur, the need to be by her side was even stronger. And what did that say about his feelings for her?

He ground his teeth together, reminding himself he had a clear view of them, at least. As a distraction, he picked up his phone and opened up a message to Jessamyn Barclay.

The idea of buying the Crooked Elm Ranch lands, but not the house, had seemed so promising he thought he'd run it by her, especially since Fleur already seemed open to the idea.

Tapping out a text, he reminded Jessamyn that his offer to buy the acreage would mean he'd take care of any citations from the local land management agencies. Surely that would make the proposal all the more appealing if they were anxious to resolve the issues. He hit Send, hoping the Barclay sisters would agree to his plan.

That way, his pledge to his parents' memory would be fulfilled, and the only thing keeping him from exploring the attraction with Fleur was an obligation to disclose a relationship to his brother.

Drake still didn't know how to do that. But Colin wouldn't be in town for the wedding for a few more days, so he still had time to figure it out. And as Fleur walked toward the truck, her meeting with Cranston apparently finished, Drake was very ready to focus on convincing her that their one night together wasn't nearly enough.

Back at Alexander Ranch an hour later, Fleur stole a sidelong glance at Drake as she walked toward a recently restored barn with him. She was still surprised to acknowledge this rugged rancher was no longer her adversary.

"Are you sure you're not hungry yet?" he asked, pausing outside the old barn.

The clean scents of pine and straw were strong here, the minimalist gray barn pretty enough to be on a magazine cover. Tall purple flowers she didn't recognize were planted on either side of the huge sliding door.

"I'd like to see the wedding venue first," she insisted, and while the answer was honest, she also knew she felt a little nervous about the evening meal she'd agreed to with Drake.

Something had shifted in his demeanor toward her since their night together. Which shouldn't surprise her, since she considered sleeping together a big step, too. And yet, she still hadn't figured out what it meant for them. What she wanted it to mean.

"Fair enough." He pivoted so that he faced her, meeting her gaze head-on. He spread his arms wide, his smile a hundred-watt level. "Prepare yourself for the site of the catering event that's going to launch your cooking career into the stratosphere."

She laughed, grateful for the moment of levity. Between the confrontation with Josiah Cranston—which had gone as well as could be expected, even if he hadn't been pleased—and the tension mounting about her evening with Drake, she appreciated the distraction.

All the more so when his nearness stirred a hunger to touch and taste him. To indulge all the pent-up longings that were part of her complicated feelings for this man.

"Let's hope you're right." Her voice sounded a little too breathless, but she tried to hide it by continuing, "The barn restoration is beautiful. I'm not surprised Emma wanted to have her wedding here."

She felt Drake's gaze linger on her a moment longer before he moved away, pushing open the huge door.

"Thank you. My father had notes for restoring everything on the ranch, from the buildings to the land. His plans emphasized sustainability and efficiency, from energy and materials to structure and design." There was a serious note in his voice that she hadn't heard before. Or maybe it was the expression on his face as he peered up at the gray timber exterior capped by a dark roof covered with solar panels on one side.

"You continued to follow your father's plans with the barn?" She found herself looking at the space with new eyes. Because she could see now that it was more than a wedding venue for Drake.

This building had been a tribute.

"Yes, I did." He stepped forward into the barn, stretching out an arm to flip on overhead lights. "His outlines were meticulous about everything from the kinds of recycled materials he wanted to use to the rainwater collection systems he envisioned for the house and barns."

Her step stuttered. "You restored other buildings, too?"

"Everything." His clipped answer somehow spoke volumes about how important that had been to him. "The house interior will be completely different from any memory you might have from when you were younger."

She hadn't been inside the Alexander home when she'd had dinner with Emma on the patio, she realized, other than to carry a few things outside from an enclosed porch.

Still, she didn't step inside the restored barn, her attention too fixated on this discovery about Drake's remodeling activity. Had his siblings minded? she wondered. How might they have felt about changes to the places in their home where they might have had special family memories? She recalled how much it meant to her to step into Gran's kitchen and have it look exactly the way she remembered.

"That must have been a tremendous undertaking." She found herself wanting to explore the whole ranch more carefully, now that she knew as much.

"And I'm not done yet." The determination in his eyes was unmistakable. "Reviving the waterway was supposed to be his crowning achievement."

Understanding dawned. His drive to buy Crooked Elm was rooted in something so much deeper than she'd imagined. Pushing her to sell hadn't simply been a way to chase her out of town or throw around his net worth. He'd wanted to fulfill his father's vision.

But before she could respond, Drake extended his hand to her. "Come on in. You should see what Emma's done in here."

When her fingers settled in the warmth of his palm, a shiver ran up her spine. She couldn't deny her connection to this man, and all at once she knew that tonight, she wasn't going to try.

She wanted to lose herself in him again, to chase the feelings that only he had ever inspired. But for now, she drew in a deep breath and entered the barn, every step, every moment of waiting ramping the desire coursing through her veins.

"Oh, how beautiful," she murmured, her gaze going upward where yards and yards of pale pink tulle wove through the rafters, creating a soft canopy dotted with white lights woven through the fabric.

Below, the reclaimed wood support beams were wound with tulle and white ribbons, like giant Maypoles. Candelabra stands were already in place around the room, the white candles protected inside tiny glass globes. On the wooden floor, rectangular tables were laid out at angles. The focus on the head table adorned with white linen and skirted with more tulle.

"There will be greenery and pink peonies on almost every surface." Drake gestured around the room with his free hand. "My job was the tulle, and Emma assured me any spots that I missed would be covered with flowers."

"You did an incredible job." She wondered what it would be like to have a brother—or even a sister—make that kind of loving effort. To have a sibling who cared so deeply about her happiness. "Emma must be thrilled."

Fleur could feel her heart beat in the palm of her hand where it rested against Drake's, her emotions swelling too big to contain. She wanted to wrap herself in the hidden kindness of this man, the generosity of spirit in someone who would make a life's work of his parents' dreams, or set everything else aside to decorate a barn for a beloved sister.

"I think so. Now you just need to come through with the food—"

Fleur touched his jaw, turning his face toward her so she could look him in the eye. Then, stretching up on her toes, she brushed a kiss over his lips. Once. Twice.

When she settled on her feet, she noticed with pleasure that his eyes remained closed for a moment afterward. He blinked them open again, heated appreciation in their depths.

"What was that for?" he asked softly, letting go of her hand to wrap his arms around her waist.

"That was my way of apologizing for ever thinking you were a bad sibling." She'd believed the worst of him for years and he hadn't deserved it.

"You can think whatever you like about me if you apologize that way," he murmured, his arms flexing in a way that brought her closer still.

"I just remembered I've actually had a lot of wicked thoughts about you over the years." She kissed his cheek and down to his jaw. Taking her time, breathing in the pine and musk scent of his skin. "Atoning thoroughly could take a while."

With a hungry groan of appreciation he backed her deeper into the building. Gently, but so very deliberately.

"In that case, I need to show you my favorite part of the restoration." He gripped one of her thighs on either side of his waist while she kept her arms around his neck. He lifted her into position.

She rocked against him, reveling in the hard

length of him all too apparent through the denim of his jeans as he walked.

"What might that be?" She paused in her kisses long enough to peer over her shoulder so she could see where he was taking her.

"We converted the old hayloft to private guest quarters since the restored barn is going to be used strictly as a place for entertaining." His long strides brought them to an open staircase at the back of the building. He began to climb the wide wooden steps, still holding her, and she could see a small landing with open doors on either side.

"Are we really going to fool around in the hayloft?" A smile pulled at her lips at the thought.

A moment later, his mouth claimed hers for a slow, thorough tasting. When he finished, she was breathing hard, growing taut with desire.

"With any luck we're going to do a whole lot more than that." Entering one of the open rooms with her still in his arms, Drake kicked the heavy door closed behind them.

Fleur's heart sped, her limbs growing heavy as she pressed herself to him. She worked her fingers under the sleeves of his T-shirt, gripping the muscles there.

"If you get these clothes off, you'd find out for yourself." She kissed along the neckline of his shirt, then licked a path underneath it to his collarbone. "But until then, my mouth can only make amends for so much."

Thirteen

Fleur saw the way her words affected him.

Drake's fingers flexed into her thighs, a raw squeeze before he lifted her off him to settle her on the white duvet in the guest bedroom. She tried to catch her breath, as she sat on the edge of the mattress, her palms smoothing over the cotton fabric encasing thick eiderdown. But it wasn't easy to steady herself while she watched Drake peel his dark T-shirt up and over his head.

Baring the hard, carved muscles of a man in his prime, his body a map she couldn't wait to explore. Behind him, the white walls and gray reclaimed wood floor faded, the man dominating everything else. Besides, she couldn't think about how much work he'd put into this place. Her heart might dissolve in a puddle of tenderness she wasn't ready to feel.

Instead, she tried to focus on the practicalities.

"Are there condoms here?" She needed to ask before she lost all focus.

A moment fast approaching when he moved his hand to the button on his jeans. She registered the ache deep inside her, a need only he could fill. Her thighs pressed together, her hands reaching for him before he'd even kicked free of the denim and boxers.

"In the bathroom. The housekeeper stocks guest amenities in here." He took her hands in his, tugging her forward as he bent closer to kiss her lips. "I'll be right back."

She hadn't even registered the words when he pulled away. It took her a moment as her eyes blinked open to understand what he'd said and where he'd gone, his broad shoulders disappearing through an open door off to one side of the room.

How was it possible she could lose herself in him—in this feeling he sparked—so thoroughly? She hadn't missed sex in the years between her first, unwise introduction to coupling and the second, toe-curling experience Drake had given her when they were together before. She'd been focused on culinary school and work.

But right now, with her fingers shaking a little as she drew off her T-shirt and reached for the snap on her jean shorts, she wondered how she could go for a week without this feeling, let alone months. Years.

She'd never known it could be this way.

And that was her last rational thought before Drake reappeared in the bedroom, his dark brown eyes lasering in on her near nakedness, his steps charging toward her like a man on a mission.

Her breath caught on a gasp, and then his arms were around her, his mouth on hers, capturing the air. She melted into him as he laid her on the bed, her limbs turning to liquid when he stretched out over her. Covering her.

His skin felt hot against hers, and she craved his warmth. His strength. The scents she associated with him filled her nostrils as his tongue stroked possessively over hers. Her hips tilted toward him, seeking more. Craving connection.

"Drake, please," she urged him faster, her hands roaming over his body to catalog the ripples of muscles and the stretch of ligaments, her fingers fascinated with every sinew and plane. "I need you."

Was it too revealing that she hungered for him this badly? No, she told herself. It was physical. A sensual appetite that could surely be appeased.

If her own passion intimidated her, at least his seemed to match it. Hooking a finger in the lace of her white thong, he dragged the insubstantial fabric down her thighs and off, leaving her in just the matching lace bra.

His hands moved to that next, though, slipping the straps down her shoulders as he kissed each nipple through the decorative cups, turning the peaks into tight points.

Then he licked a path through the valley between

her breasts, flicking open the fastening there with one finger so he could feast on her hungrily.

All the while she arched and writhed against him, wanting to feel him inside her.

When she reached between them to stroke over his erection from base to tip, the ragged growl he made sent thrills through her.

"You don't make it easy for me to take my time with you, do you?" He asked the question as he kissed his way back up her chest to her throat and along her jaw to her ear, where he nipped the lobe gently.

A shiver tripped down her spine.

"I've thought about this too many times since we were together last," she admitted, the words tumbling out with zero filters. It couldn't be helped, though.

Something inside her had been unleashed, and she couldn't seem to call it back now.

"You're all I've thought about, Fleur," he rasped out between kisses, and she took his face in her hand to steer his mouth to hers, wanting to drink in what he'd said. To taste the need on her tongue and savor it.

The greedy way he kissed her, the press of his hips against hers underscored his words. She reached blindly around the bed for the condom and unwrapped the package, her fingers fumbling but fueled by desire.

"Let me." He took the condom from her, sheathing himself in one easy move before he levered up to sit on the edge of the bed, taking her with him.

For a moment, she wasn't sure where he wanted her, but then he lifted her onto his lap to straddle him. Their eyes met. Held.

When he lifted her again, he positioned her right where she needed to be so that she sank down, down and deeper down onto him. The feeling was perfect, filling her completely, so that she wanted to stay there forever.

Except then Drake moved, and she realized that was exactly what she needed. Her legs locked around him while his hips withdrew and then pistoned forward. Again and again.

Each thrust took her higher. Every moment of sharing her body with him seemed to tangle him in her heart. Deeper and deeper.

The thought was a dangerous one, but it was as inescapable as the release shimmering just out of reach. So close.

"Fleur." His breath stirred her hair, the word soft and passionate as any prayer. "Let go with me. Feel me."

For a moment, she met his intense gaze and everything inside her stopped. Held. Even time seemed to slow.

Then her orgasm crashed over her, her feminine muscles contracting and releasing in lush spasms that seemed to shake her whole body. As if from far away, she felt Drake tensing, every part of him going taut while she convulsed through the sweetness of her release. And then he was right there with her, his shout of satisfaction making her thighs clamp him tighter.

Bliss.

There was no other word for the sensual perfection of the moment, and Fleur let it fill her up as she slumped against him, his shoulder anchoring her where she rested her forehead for long minutes afterward.

Slowly, reason returned. It was almost disorienting to come back to the guest bedroom in the restored barn, to recognize how completely she'd lost her senses to this man and what they'd shared. She remembered how it had been the same way with him the first time, and she'd had to ask for a reprieve in discussing what their relationship meant.

And here she was again, still not ready to talk to him about that. Even though now, she feared she understood all too well what she was feeling.

Somehow, despite all her best intentions, she'd fallen in love with Drake Alexander.

Tensing at the realization, she wondered if she'd be able to hide it from him. She had to, of course. Drake hadn't even wanted her to stay in Catamount when she'd first told him about her wish to remain here.

His new idea of trying to buy the lands while she and her sisters kept the house hadn't been formed with any hope of having a relationship with her, either. He'd just wanted to fulfill his father's wishes.

"Hey." Drake shifted beneath her, his shoulder moving in a way that made her straighten to face him. "Everything okay?"

No. She was in complete and utter crisis.

She was in love.

But she swallowed down the unwise thoughts and forced a smile.

"That was amazing." She settled on a true statement that would have to do for now. "I was just trying to recover my senses."

For a moment, his dark eyes searched hers, as if he could tell there was more at work than what she'd confessed. But in the end, he nodded.

"Me, too. But I'm still going to make you dinner." He stroked one hand through her hair, her braid having fallen out at some point without her even realizing. He sifted through the waves now, gently untangling the strands. "You'll feel good as new after that."

Fleur wasn't so sure about that, but until she could contemplate her next move, she just reached for her clothes. She needed some kind of barrier between them before her feelings became all too apparent.

Something had shifted between them.

Drake could feel their equilibrium was all off-balance even though they shared a nice meal. His steaks had turned out perfectly, the side dishes simple but well cooked. And while he knew that Fleur was a professional chef, he didn't think the food had been that much of a disappointment.

If anything, she'd seemed genuinely pleased that he'd gone to the effort of cooking for her.

No, there was something else brewing between them. As he finished putting away the leftovers in the double-sized refrigerator, he stole a glance at Fleur where she wiped down the white quartz countertop where they'd eaten.

"I appreciate you letting me use this kitchen as a home base for catering the wedding," she remarked as she walked toward him. She rinsed out the dishcloth before squeezing out the excess water and draping it over the divider between the stainless steel sinks. "It's so roomy, and the appliances are a caterer's dream."

She ran a finger over the knobs at the industrial-sized gas stove when her cell phone chimed. Hesitating, she glanced his way.

"Feel free to take that," he encouraged her as he closed the refrigerator door. "I can step into the next room if you need privacy."

Withdrawing her phone from her pocket, she checked the screen. "No need. It's Jessamyn."

Fleur lowered herself into one of the counter stools at the island, where they'd eaten.

"Hello?" she answered the call, her gray eyes flicking to his while Jessamyn spoke for a minute.

For a moment, he wondered if her sister was calling with good news for them both—that she liked the idea of selling Drake the Crooked Elm Ranch acreage while the Barclay sisters kept the house.

But as he moved closer to the island to take a seat beside Fleur, he could tell that it wasn't good news. At first, a line appeared between her eyebrows, a confused furrow. But then, as her sister continued to speak, her jaw went slack with surprise.

"Are you serious?" Her breathing quickened as she shot up out of her seat. She appeared agitated as she paced around the island. "Can Dad even do that?"

Drake tensed, not liking to see her unhappy. His protective instincts fired, and he stood, too. Not that he could take action until he knew what was wrong, but he hated for her to be upset.

What had her father done?

He moved to close the distance between them, instinctively wanting to offer comfort. But just before he reached her, Fleur's shoulders tightened, and her mouth compressed into a thin, flat line.

Worse? Her gray eyes lifted to meet his. And he could have sworn all that anger was directed at… him?

"What is it?" he asked, feeling involved somehow in her conversation, even though she still held the phone to her ear.

But Fleur didn't answer him. Still locking gazes with him, she spoke again into the phone.

"Jess, I have Drake with me right now. If I put you on speaker, would you please repeat that so he knows?"

Worry speared through him as Fleur stabbed a button on her screen.

"Of course." Jessamyn's brusque tone came through the speaker as Fleur held the device between them. "I was just telling Fleur that our father intercepted Drake's message to me about wanting to buy the Crooked Elm rangelands. He's noticed Drake's interest in the property, apparently, both at Gran's memorial and then with the follow-up call and text about buying the parcel even with the citations pending. Now Dad thinks maybe those acres are worth more than he realized."

Drake shook his head, not understanding what was wrong.

"Does he think I should offer more for them?" he asked, unsure what he was missing. "I can increase my offer."

Why was Fleur so angry?

"Tell him," Fleur said, her words as sharp as any she'd shot at him when they'd been enemies. "Explain what his need to force his own agenda has led to."

On the other end of the call, Jessamyn continued in that clipped business tone. Yet there was no mistaking the steely anger beneath it.

"Money isn't the issue. Now our father is contesting Antonia's will, Drake. It could be tied up in probate court for months. Or more. Bottom line, you won't be able to buy the land anyway until the case is settled."

The news devastated him. So he understood it had to devastate Fleur one hundred times as much. His gut sank.

"Fleur, I'm so sorry." He wanted to comfort her. To find a way to bear the news that must be crushing to her. "There must be some way—"

"There isn't." She snapped, her eyes flinty with anger before they moved away from him and back to her phone. "Jessamyn, I appreciate the update. Do you think I'm even legally allowed to live there?"

Drake speared his fingers through his hair, unable to believe what he was hearing. How could Mateo do this to his daughters?

"You should be fine since you were already there before Dad contested the will. But in yet more bad news, Josiah Cranston legally doesn't have to vacate the property now until probate is cleared."

Hell. Anger coursed through his veins even as Drake knew he had no right to it. Fleur and her sisters were the ones who deserved to be furious about this.

"It's a lot to absorb at once," Fleur said finally, her voice shaking slightly. "I'll call you later once I get my head around this, okay?"

"Sure thing, Fleur," Jessamyn returned, sounding exhausted as she heaved out a small sigh. "I'll get in touch with Lark."

Fleur disconnected and tucked the phone into her pocket, her movements deliberate. Slow.

Still, he recalled how her voice had a tremor in it a moment ago.

"I'm so sorry," he repeated, his hands landing on her shoulders. "We can hire an attorney who specializes in probate—"

"We?" Her voice rose an octave as she glared at him before spinning away from his touch. "*We* aren't doing anything together, Drake." She removed the place mats from the counter and replaced them in a buffet drawer, her movements abrupt. Jerky. "This is a problem for my sisters and me to deal with. It's not one you can manage with money and influence. In fact, it doesn't have anything to do with you."

His brain worked fast to try to follow what she was angry at him for, but the pieces didn't add up.

"Fleur, it's not my fault your father contested the will."

"Oh no?" She fisted her hands and settled them on her hips, the emotion practically steaming off her as she faced him. "Did you miss the part where my sister said your interest in the land made our money-hungry dad want to get involved? You're so gung ho to buy it that of course my big shot real estate developer father wants to know if he can make a buck on it."

He knew she was upset, and she had every reason to be. So he told himself not to argue with her. But damn it, how could he allow her to think the worst of him when he hadn't done anything but try to help?

"I couldn't have possibly known that he would view my interest that way. I only spoke to Jessamyn about it, not him."

Hadn't they been in bed together just a few hours ago? He'd shared more with her than any other woman. So it shredded him to see her look at him now as if he'd hurt her on purpose.

"Right. You spoke to my sister because you couldn't wait for me to do that, even though I'm back in Catamount to find some kind of peace among my siblings again. Why couldn't you just allow me to work at my own pace to settle things? I invited them here this summer so that we could talk face–to-face, but that wasn't good enough for you. Why did your wants have to come first?" She spoke faster with each sentence, her hurt more and more evident.

Her eyes shone with unshed tears, and he sensed the need to do something, say something, to fix things. Fast.

"They didn't. I hoped that I was helping you at the same time I was helping myself." He wasn't the bad guy here, but damned if he could make her see that.

"Did you really?" She folded her arms, her shoulders practically vibrating with her anger. "Or did you tell yourself that to justify throwing your money around to get what you wanted?"

Was that true?

The idea sat uncomfortably on him for a moment.

"If that's what I did, I promise you it was never my intention to hurt you." His heart pounded as if he needed any reminders that he was screwing this up. Saying all the wrong things.

She shook her head, taking a step back and grabbing her purse. "Too late. And your big offer isn't going to get you what you wanted this time anyway, so all your efforts to speed things up were for nothing."

"Fleur, wait." He followed her toward the door, unwilling to see her walk away upset. "Let's talk about this—"

"No." She held her ground in the hall entrance, pausing long enough to make sure he understood that much. "We won't be talking about this, or anything else, either. I'll be here for Emma's wedding, but I have no interest in seeing you then or at any other time."

The words pummeled him harder than any thrashing he'd ever taken in the bull riding arena. And they sure as hell made him feel worse than any fall.

But as if that weren't bad enough, she punctuated them by turning on her heel and walking out the door.

Fourteen

Every day that passed without Fleur in his life hurt more than the one before.

Standing outside Emma's wedding reception as the sun dropped out of sight beyond the trees, Drake regarded the festivities in the hope of catching sight of Fleur as she catered the reception. A local band played upbeat country music inside the barn, the main doors both swung open so that guests could enjoy cocktails outside, too. White lights canopied the outdoor bar and a few tables were set up for guests who wished to take a breather from the dancing indoors. A bonfire burned in a firepit nearby, the flames ready for later in the evening when there would be s'more roasting for the kids.

Everything looked perfect. His parents' dreams

for this day were fulfilled to the letter, and he felt good about that. But inside, everything seemed wrong. He hadn't spoken to his brother beyond the most superficial of greetings.

And worse, he hadn't seen Fleur.

He'd seen signs of her presence everywhere today. From the thoughtful favors she'd created for Emma with bags of spiced nuts for all the guests, to the abundant buffet table stacked with the Spanish tapas she specialized in making, Fleur's influence was all around him. And yet, she'd remained so thoroughly in the background that he'd never caught a single glimpse of her. Was she avoiding him? Did she even care enough to feel that strong of an emotion for him? Or was she just…indifferent? That possibility stung the most.

Even now his gaze went down to the main house where the kitchen lights were visible from the barn. She'd hired helpers who carried fresh trays up from the kitchen and took away the empties. Allowing her to stay firmly in the background.

An unexpected voice rumbled low behind him. "Dad and Mom would be proud to see this day."

Shaking off his thoughts, Drake turned to find Colin approach from the shadows. Clad in a tux and black Stetson just like his own, the two men looked similar enough on the outside. Yet how different were they inside when they'd barely spoken in years beyond the occasional necessary exchange about family business.

And that *was* his fault. Drake might not agree with

Fleur's assessment of his mistakes where she was concerned. But he couldn't deny that he'd done his brother a grave disservice five years ago when he'd insisted Fleur break things off with him. It pained him to admit that now. Especially when acknowledging as much to Colin could drive his brother to seek Fleur again.

The possibility sent a crushing weight down onto his solar plexus.

"Glen is a good man," Drake acknowledged, trying to get a read on Colin. "I think Mom and Dad would approve."

"I don't mean Glen." Colin shook his head as he leaned against the trunk of a small cherry tree. "I mean the ranch. The barns. The land. It all looks just like what Dad wanted to accomplish."

A couple of older kids ran past them in their wedding finery carrying sparklers, an early nod to the fireworks planned for later when the sky fully darkened.

"You think so?" Drake wasn't fishing for compliments from his brother. He knew Colin wouldn't BS him about that of all things. "There were times I questioned the plans, wishing I could just ask him what he wanted—"

The emotion that rose in his throat made it necessary to cut himself off. Normally, he was good about tucking those old hurts away, but on Emma's wedding day, standing beside his long-estranged brother, he felt the full weight of the mistakes he'd made as head of the family.

"I wish I could ask him things, too. Both of them." Colin scuffed his dress boots through the grass. "Being home makes me wish that all the more."

Drake looked up fast at that. "Is this still home for you? I haven't spoiled that?"

"In spite of everything, yes, I guess it is." Colin tipped his hat back farther on his head as he rocked on his heels. "Montana is nice, and I'm not returning here anytime soon. But I'll always think of this place as home."

Drake's throat closed at the thought of his brother never around for more than the occasional wedding. The country music and the laugher from inside the barn seemed miles away as he dug deep to make a long-overdue apology.

"I'm sorry to hear that you're not coming back. All the more so because it's my fault you left. I had no right to interfere with you when you wanted to marry." He couldn't bring himself to say *when you wanted to marry Fleur*. Because he couldn't even put their names together in his head without pain spiking throughout him.

"Your fault?" Colin shook his head, seeming genuinely surprised. "For what, saying the obvious that Fleur Barclay and I would never work in a million years? Don't think I didn't know that, brother."

Reeling, Drake swept off his hat and scratched a hand through his hair, sifting through his brother's words. He wanted to make sure he wasn't just hearing what he wished to hear.

"I thought you were furious with me for asking her to end the engagement." He knew Fleur had blamed him. Deservedly so.

"Hell no. I was furious with myself for hurting her in the first place when she and I—we were never going to be more than friends." Colin turned a tortured expression his way, his eyes pained. "All this time, I thought you knew. I was ashamed I went after her when I knew you liked her."

What? Had he been that obvious?

"Me?" He felt like someone had pulled the rug out from under him. He was left standing upright, but he wasn't quite sure how. "Why would you think that when we couldn't even stand to be around one another?"

Even as he spoke the words, Colin's eyes shot heavenward. "It's one thing to kid yourself, Drake, but you're not fooling me. Then, or now. You've always liked Fleur. From the time you assigned yourself as her personal protector at every rodeo, chasing guys away with bared teeth, to when you nearly took my head off for sleeping with her."

Drake bristled, his fingers fisting. And if just *hearing* those words did that to him—maybe his brother had a point.

He swore softly under his breath.

"I hated myself even before you came home and found out about us." Colin tipped his head to look at the sky where an early firework from a far-off neighbor sparkled red through the night.

"Let's say for argument's sake that I did have feelings for Fleur." Did? The reality of his feelings was staring him in the face every time he stared at the kitchen windows down the hill and willed himself to catch a glimpse of her.

He loved Fleur.

Deeply. Passionately. And his brother had known it long before he had.

"All right," his brother agreed. "We'll say that."

"Why would you be with her? I know we didn't always see eye to eye, but I thought we got along well enough."

Colin's dark eyebrows shot together as he frowned. "It had more to do with me than you. I resented you too much for having your life together while I was always struggling in your shadow. I missed having a brother once you decided to step into Dad's shoes and you called all the shots around here. You name it, I pinned it on you."

A burst of laughter from inside the barn reminded Drake he should return to the reception soon. Share this day with Emma. And yet, he'd waited half a lifetime for this conversation with his brother. He couldn't walk away from it now.

"I've only just started to realize that I may be more controlling than I should be."

"May be?" his brother said with the quirk of an eyebrow.

Drake shrugged sheepishly. He recalled Fleur's words too well about pushing his own agenda. And for what? He'd only hurt her by not giving her space to work through the legalities of the ranch inheritance in her own way. "And for that matter, I've also only started to understand that I have feelings for Fleur." His heart felt full. Heavy with the knowledge he needed to share.

"I love her," Drake admitted. "And I've been as hard-headed and blind with her as I have been with you."

Another firework exploded silently from some distant point, the shimmer of yellow and green lights flashing across the sky.

Colin straightened from where he'd leaned against the cherry tree and clapped a heavy hand on Drake's shoulder.

"If I've learned one thing in the past five years, it's that it's never too late to make better choices. Starting my own spread forced me to be my own man." Colin nodded toward the building that housed the kitchen where Fleur worked. "I apologized to Fleur tonight for the mistakes I made in the past, and it felt good to know there were no hard feelings."

Colin had already spoken to Fleur? Drake turned his gaze to the kitchen window once more, understanding that his whole life—his future—was inside that room right now. He needed to go down there and tell her as much, whether or not she forgave him.

He wouldn't allow this argument to fester for five years the way he'd done with Colin.

"Thank you." Not sure what else to say, he wrapped his brother in a hug. "And this is always your home."

Colin squeezed his shoulder before letting go. "Good. Then I will be the representative Alexander male of the hour, while you go patch things up with Fleur."

"Deal." Feeling lighter than he had in years, Drake smiled. He knew he had a long way to go to heal things with his sibling, but tonight was a start. And it felt damned good to have Colin here again.

He just hoped he could express himself to Fleur more effectively than he had in the past. He couldn't control whether or not she wanted him in her life. But he could make certain she understood how much he loved her, and he wasn't leaving that kitchen until he'd made his point.

Staring through the window at the silver lights exploding in a starfish pattern over the creek, Fleur chastised herself for being too chicken to leave the kitchen to go outside and enjoy the Fourth of July display.

Plus, she was still feeling emotional from her earlier encounter with Colin. They'd managed to talk, express their sorrow over the loss of their child, and come to terms with their relationship. She felt a pang as she realized her feelings for Colin had never been deep or strong or complicated. He'd been a safety net for her, and she a rebellion against his brother's rules for him. They'd parted on a good note.

So far, only the lights from neighboring ranches had arced across the sky. But Emma and Glen had a show planned for dusk, a newlywed celebration to cap off their wedding day. There'd been a time when

Fleur might have imagined her enjoying that moment with Drake beside her.

But after their fight last week—after the way he'd flexed his financial might hoping to make the sale of Crooked Elm happen faster—she had told him she didn't want to see him anymore. As much as it hurt to think of not being with him again, she also knew herself well enough to understand she couldn't spend her life feeling like her wishes were secondary to a man with money. Her father had made her feel less than enough for one lifetime.

Now she made her own decisions. Called her own shots.

And it was a lonely battle to have won.

The one bright moment was the talk she'd had with Colin. They were better as friends, they'd agreed. And she felt a weight off her mind thinking about that. Her conscience was eased regarding her past with Colin. They'd forgiven each other.

Returning to the counter, she stacked up the cleaned serving trays and slid them into their canvas carrying case. The evening had seemed like a success even though she hadn't visited the reception herself yet. And she needed to, soon. Emma deserved her personal congratulations.

When a side door opened, she expected to see Marta walk into the room with another empty tray. But when she looked up, Drake stood before her.

Dressed in a tuxedo and black Stetson, he had a pink rose boutonniere. She'd never seen him so devastatingly handsome, although she suspected it had more to do with how long it had been since she'd seen him than with what he wore.

"Fleur." He spoke her name like an answer to all his questions.

And it hurt her because she knew that wasn't the case.

"Does the bride need something?" she asked, channeling Jessamyn and turning on her business mode. "I can send Marta up with more *croquetas*."

She bustled toward the refrigerator, willing herself not to think about how handsome Drake looked. Or about what he might want.

Or how much she wanted him.

"Emma doesn't need anything," Drake asserted, stepping deeper into the room while still maintaining some distance. "The food was incredible and all the guests are singing your praises while they dance."

She really would have liked to have overseen things personally, so she appreciated hearing that. She'd stayed away to safeguard her heart. And keep from causing a scene.

"I'm glad to hear it." She thought of the heavy apron she wore. That her hair was in a net in deference to the food prep. Swiftly, she withdrew the net and untied the apron.

Because the cooking was finished, of course. Not because Drake stood there looking so good it made her hurt.

She tucked the items into her duffel bag and ran a self-conscious hand over her matted hair.

"You look beautiful." His low voice curled

through her like smoke wisps as his gaze roamed over her yellow tea-length dress, the tulle skirt embroidered with daisies.

Swallowing her nerves, she tucked her hands under her elbows, folding her arms tightly.

"I know you're not here to talk about that. What can I do for you?"

"Emma wanted me to make sure you didn't miss the fireworks." He tugged off his Stetson and set it on a counter stool. "But that's only half the truth. I realized that I need to make better choices with you if I want any chance of convincing you not to walk away from what's happening between us."

Irritation flared.

"Isn't that how we got here in the first place? You making all the choices?" She'd had days to think about what had happened between them and she still felt frustrated. Resentful. "I understand you didn't mean to undermine me by going directly to my sister, Drake. But that's how it felt to me. And I'm extremely sensitive to that after the way my father played god with his financial power."

"I overstepped," he acknowledged, his expression disconsolate. "I took it for granted that you would want help, and I thought I was helping. In hindsight, I can see that I had no business assuming that. But I've accomplished a lot charging ahead without asking anyone's permission, and I failed to notice that it hurts people I care about."

"People?" Curiosity prompted her to ask.

Especially now that she noticed the violet shadows under his eyes. Almost as if he'd lost as much sleep this week as she had.

"You. And Colin, too." He flicked open the button on his tuxedo jacket before dipping a finger into his bow tie and loosening that as well. "We spoke just now, and I realized that what I perceived as being protective has been viewed as domineering to those around me."

Her heart softened a fraction at the despairing note in his voice.

"Colin said that?" She found her thoughts returning to the time she'd spent with him. They'd always been friends, their interactions easy and fun, unlike the way she and Drake had sparked friction.

Those weeks she and Colin had dated, she remembered him complaining that Drake was hard to live with, his expectations too high for anyone to meet. At the time, she'd thought she'd understood since she had her own strained relationships with Lark and Jessamyn. But maybe the fractures had gone deeper between the brothers.

"Apparently, he left for Montana because of it." His dark eyes met hers. "Or at least, that was one of his reasons. But it made me realize that I don't want to be that man who thinks he knows best. I didn't see the damage I was doing by getting involved in your business, Fleur, but I can change."

There was an earnestness in his voice, a depth of concern that she hadn't heard before.

It awakened her empathy. Her hope.

"Anyone can *change*," she agreed, her heart hammering so loudly it was all she heard. "If they want to. If it really means something to them."

How many times had she thought that about her family? All the Barclays had laughed at her attempts at peacekeeping in their dysfunctional clan, but she was still idealistic enough to believe people could change if they cared enough to try. Her failures hadn't taken that away from her.

And this was the first time anyone she'd loved had suggested they wanted to change.

"Fleur." Drake moved closer to her now, his dark cowboy boots covering the steps between them so that he stood before her. He lifted one of her hands and held it between both of his. "I love you. And I can't think of any more compelling reason in the world to change than for love."

The warmth of his touch anchored her as her heart soared on those words. Because coming from Drake Alexander, she knew it wasn't merely a phrase to toss out lightly. She'd seen firsthand how he kept his pledges to his parents.

Her chest expanded, a joy exploding inside it like the fireworks she'd seen through the kitchen window. Yet before she could speak, he continued.

"I know that I don't deserve you. Not yet." His dark eyes were serious. Somber. He squeezed her hands lightly, his voice lowering. "But if you'll give me a chance, I am confident that I can show you that you mean everything in the world to me."

Something shifted inside her, a new tenderness opening wide that gave her a different perspective of him. No doubt he was a man of strong principle and fierce loyalty. And now, he wanted to envelop her in all of those deep feelings.

A relationship with Drake promised her a depth of love—and passion—unlike anything she'd ever experienced before.

"I love you, too, Drake. So much." She spoke the words aloud that had been circling around her thoughts every hour since they'd been together last, and it felt beautiful to share.

He crushed her to him, holding her tightly. And she knew without question that he'd been as frantically worried about losing her as she'd been about him. She understand that desperate hug because it echoed everything inside her. She sighed into him.

And it felt like coming home.

"I will always want to fix everything I can for you," he spoke the words through her hair, kissing her in between words. "But you can tell me when I can't, and I promise that I will listen."

The last of her worries fell away, her heart full and so very happy. A smile curved her lips, the rightness of the moment filling her whole being.

"I will hold you to that," she told him simply, leaning back to look him in the eyes, this proud, hardworking rancher that she loved.

And he stared at her like she'd solved all his problems. His eyes held a wealth of tenderness, and she wanted to melt right into it.

"I'm going to do everything I can to make you happy, you know." He stroked his hand over her cheek, slowing the touch so he could trace her lips with his thumb.

Her knees went weak from just that caress.

Although knowing he loved her might have had a little to do with the way she felt weightless and buoyantly joyful.

"I like the sound of that. I hope it involves you cooking for me again."

"It means standing behind you with whatever you decide to do. Offering advice when you need it. Letting you fight your battles with your father but being a sounding board when you want it. Whatever you and your sisters decide to do, you'll have my full support."

His eyes lit with promise as the sound of fireworks exploded outside over the creek. Up at the barn, the wedding guests cheered.

She knew they needed to join Emma and celebrate her wedding, but Drake held her there a moment longer.

"I'm going to do so much more than that," he vowed. "And when you want to start a restaurant, I hope you'll keep in mind that I just happen to have one."

She laughed, dizzy with the promise of the life they could share together. There were still problems ahead. Things that needed to be resolved with her sisters and their legacy from their grandmother. But knowing that this man was in her corner was a dream come true.

"I'll keep it in mind. For now, we'd better go

watch the fireworks." Taking his hand, she tugged him toward the side door. "This is the perfect time to celebrate a happily-ever-after."

"I like the sound of that," he said in her ear, right before he swept her off her feet and into his arms. "Almost as much as I'm going to like calling you *Mrs.* Silver Spurs."

* * * * *

Don't miss a single
Return to Catamount novel
by USA TODAY *bestselling author*
Joanne Rock!

Rocky Mountain Rivals
One Colorado Night
A Colorado Claim

Available exclusively from
Harlequin Desire.

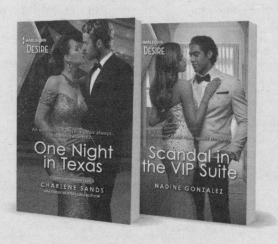

#2881 ON OPPOSITE SIDES
Texas Cattleman's Club: Ranchers and Rivals
by Cat Schield
Determined to save her family ranch, Chelsea Grandin launches a daring scheme to seduce Nolan Thurston to discover his family's plans—and he does the same. Although they suspect they're using one another, their schemes disintegrate as attraction takes over...

#2882 ONE COLORADO NIGHT
Return to Catamount • by Joanne Rock
Cutting ties with her family, developer Jessamyn Barclay returns to the ranch to make peace, not expecting to see her ex, Ryder Wakefield. When one hot night changes everything, will they reconnect for their baby's sake or will a secret from the past ruin everything?

#2883 AFTER HOURS TEMPTATION
404 Sound • by Kianna Alexander
Focused on finishing an upcoming album, sound engineer Teagan Woodson and guitarist Maxton McCoy struggle to keep things professional as their attraction grows. But agreeing to "just a fling" may lead to *everything* around them falling apart...

#2884 WHEN THE LIGHTS GO OUT...
Angel's Share • by Jules Bennett
A blackout at her distillery leaves straitlaced Elise Hawthorne in the dark with her potential new client, restaurateur Antonio Rodriguez. One kiss leads to more, but everything is on the line when the lights come back on...

#2885 AN OFFER FROM MR. WRONG
Cress Brothers • by Niobia Bryant
Desperately needing a buffer between him and his newly discovered family, chef and reluctant heir Lincoln Cress turns to the one person who's all wrong for him—the PI who uncovered this information, Bobbie Barnett. But this fake relationship reveals very real desire...

#2886 HOW TO FAKE A WEDDING DATE
Little Black Book of Secrets • by Karen Booth
Infamous for canceling her million-dollar nuptials, Alexandra Gold is having a *little* trouble finding a date to the wedding of the season. Enter her brother's best friend, architect Ryder Carson. He's off-limits, so he's *safe*—except for the undeniable sparks between them!

YOU CAN FIND MORE INFORMATION ON UPCOMING HARLEQUIN TITLES, FREE EXCERPTS AND MORE AT HARLEQUIN.COM.

HDCNM0522

Welcome to Four Corners Ranch, Maisey Yates's newest miniseries, where the West is still wild...and when a cowboy needs a wife, he decides to find her the old-fashioned way!

Evelyn Moore can't believe she's agreed to uproot her city life to become Oregon cowboy and single dad Sawyer Garrett's mail-order bride. Her love for his tiny daughter is instant. Her feelings for Sawyer are...more complicated. Her gruff cowboy husband ignites a thrilling desire in her, but Sawyer is determined to keep their marriage all about the baby. But what happens if Evelyn wants it all?

The front door opened, and a man came out. He had on a black cowboy hat, and he was holding a baby. Those were the first two details she took in, but then there was... Well, there was the whole rest of him.

Evelyn could feel his eyes on her from some fifty feet away, could see the piercing blue color. His nose was straight and strong, as was his jaw. His lips were remarkable, and she didn't think she had ever really found lips on a man all that remarkable. He had the sort of symmetrical good looks that might make a man almost too pretty, but he was saved from that by a scar that edged through the corner of his mouth, creating a thick white line that disrupted the symmetry there. He was tall. Well over six feet, and broad.

And his arms were...

Good Lord.

He was wearing a short-sleeved black T-shirt, and he cradled the tiny baby in the crook of a massive bicep and forearm. He could easily lift bales of hay and throw them around. Hell, he could probably easily lift the truck and throw it around.

He was beautiful. Objectively, absolutely beautiful.

But there was something more than that. Because as he walked toward her, she felt like he was stealing increments of her breath, emptying her lungs. She'd seen handsome men before. She'd been around celebrities who were touted as the sexiest men on the planet.

But she had never felt anything quite like this.

Because this wasn't just about how he looked on the outside, though it was sheer masculine perfection; it was about what he did to her insides. Like he had taken the blood in her veins and replaced it with fire. And she could say with absolute honesty she had never once in all of her days wanted to grab a stranger and fling herself at him, and push them both into the nearest closet, bedroom, whatever, and…

Well, everything.

But she felt it, right then and there with him.

And there was something about the banked heat in his blue eyes that made her think he might feel exactly the same way.

And suddenly she was terrified of all the freedom. Giddy with it, which went right along with that joy/terror paradox from before.

She didn't know anyone here. She had come without anyone's permission or approval. She was just here. With this man. And there was nothing to stop them from…anything.

Except he was holding a baby and his sister was standing right to her left. But otherwise…

She really hoped that he was Sawyer. Because if he was Wolf, it was going to be awkward.

"Evelyn," he said. And goose bumps broke out over her arms. And she knew. Because he was the same man who had told her that she would be making him meat loaf whether she liked it or not.

And suddenly the reason it had felt distinctly sexual this time became clear.

"Yes," she responded.

"Sawyer," he said. "Sawyer Garrett." And then he absurdly took a step forward and held his hand out. To shake. And she was going to have to… touch him. Touch him and not melt into a puddle at his feet.

Find out what happens next in Evelyn and Sawyer's marriage deal in Unbridled Cowboy, *the unmissable first installment in Maisey Yates's new Four Corners Ranch miniseries.*

Don't miss Unbridled Cowboy *by New York Times bestselling author Maisey Yates, available May 2022 wherever HQN books and ebooks are sold.*

HQNBooks.com

PHMYEXP0522

Get 4 FREE REWARDS!

We'll send you 2 FREE Books plus 2 FREE Mystery Gifts.

FREE Value Over **$20**

Both the **Harlequin® Desire** and **Harlequin Presents®** series feature compelling novels filled with passion, sensuality and intriguing scandals.